A Dying Fall

A Dying Fall

A
MYSTERY NOVEL
By Hildegarde Dolson

J. B. Lippincott Company

Philadelphia and New York

For Dick

1

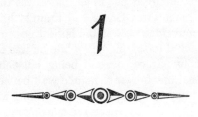

As Lucy Ramsdale said when the news reached her, "If Grace's papa could hear this, he wouldn't turn over in his grave—he'd levitate."

Grace Dilworth's papa was buried under the largest marble edifice in Wingate's cemetery, but anybody who had tangled with Sam Dilworth wouldn't have quite put it past him to crack through a marble tombstone and commandeer a passing hearse. He had been a very forcible man. And he had kept his daughter in loving thralldom from the time she'd teethed on his platinum cuff links. Grace had been thirty-nine when he died, and the betting was that, when she went off on a long cruise afterward, she was still, as Lucy put it, "untouched by human hands."

If Grace had come home from her trip with an ocelot or a two-foot pygmy, it wouldn't have caused much talk. The people of Wingate, Connecticut (population seven thousand, not counting masochistic summer commuters), took oddities in stride. But Grace Dilworth had not come home with an ocelot or a pygmy; she had brought home a six-foot man and was keeping him right on the premises. According to the best reckoning—and Wingate ladies were very shrewd at this sort of higher mathematics—he was at least six years younger than his hostess.

In some ways, Lucy Ramsdale had been pleased to hear about Grace's acquisition, because she believed passionately, almost primitively, that no woman could be liberated without a man.

But what annoyed her slightly was that she had had other plans for Grace, involving Lucy's new tenant, Inspector James Mc-Dougal. What annoyed her much more was that she hadn't yet met Grace's man. True, Grace had brought him home only five days before, but since he was the hottest gossip item in Wingate, Lucy had wanted to sample him while he was fresh. If she found him suitable for Grace, beyond being tall enough—she had already seen that much over the stone wall between the two properties—then Lucy was magnanimously willing to forego her plans to merge Grace and the inspector in matrimony.

In this spirit, she had phoned and invited her neighbor over for drinks: "Bring your houseguest. Are you going to marry him?" She was old enough to say whatever she wanted to, although age had very little to do with it. She had usually said what she wanted to, from the age of eleven months on.

Men seldom objected to Lucy's frankness. She had been a beauty, and now, in her sixties, she still had the finely whittled bones, the flash and fire—and sometimes the imperious ways—of an indestructible belle. But not a Southern belle; Lucy was much too direct. Women were more put off by this than men. Grace Dilworth had shied away from the head-on frankness of "Are you going to marry him?" And she had gone on to commit the unforgivable (to Lucy) stupidity of refusing the invitation with top-of-the-tongue phrases like "take a rain check." One did NOT take a rain check for a command performance. Lucy, a solipsist, took a dim view of this.

From where she sat on her terrace, that unseasonably hot June afternoon, she could very well have seen the two tall figures taking turns on the diving board of the Dilworths' mammoth swimming pool. But she didn't see them because she had tugged her chair around so that her back was haughtily to the wall.

In Lucy's mind, there was a vast difference between being nosy and being healthily curious. Nosy women pushed in where they weren't wanted and were hard to snub. Lucy was used to being wanted, and as for being snubbed, it had happened to her so rarely that her pride was still vibrating from Grace's casual turndown. She had none of the introvert's need to creep off and lick her wounds in brooding privacy. She had been happily married for almost forty years and a widow for only three. Any prolonged solitude, when she wasn't working or sleeping, affected her like the itch.

By shifting her eyes to the left—front left—she could see her tenant, Inspector McDougal, in the cutting garden beside the driveway. He was burying mothballs around plants, on the theory that this discouraged cutworms. Lucy had already told him it was a damn silly waste of time, as silly as dunking tulip bulbs in castor oil to discourage mice. Now she sat in the shade of her giant maple and seethed because he was out in the broiling sun doing this senseless thing when he might be sitting comfortably chatting with her. The fact that there wasn't as much shade as usual, because the cankerworms had had a green feast and the new leaves were inching back so slowly, made her seethe all the more.

She got up suddenly, walked to the front edge of the flagstone terrace, and yelled. For a woman who looked as delicate as fine porcelain, she would have made a surprisingly good hog caller. "Mac, get the hell out of that sun."

Inspector McDougal's answer came in a mild but infuriatingly clear tone, "I haven't finished yet."

Lucy considered going out to the cutting garden, but she was already dressed for the three o'clock meeting at the Dilworth Arts and Crafts Center, and she was wearing white linen sandals that didn't mix well with pungently fertilized dirt. She was also pragmatist enough to know that if the inspector wanted to finish what he was doing, he would finish it. And he almost never worked and talked at the same time. As for titillating gossip, he had none. If he was told a delicious bit of rumor, it seemed to bounce off his tall, thin frame like a tennis ball off a pole. Lucy had reason to know he absorbed whatever he heard and chewed on it, but what she craved now was some back-and-forth chatter.

She went in from the terrace, banging the screen door expressively, and through the airy big living room to the phone on the table in the hall. She and Hal had bought the little mahogany tiered table right after they moved to the country, at Wingate's

Way Back Antiques shop, laughing over what Hal called the rich Regency redundancy. Remembering that, her eyes prickled with tears, and she dabbed them away impatiently, in order to see to dial the number. She wanted to catch Alec Foster, her neighbor down the road, before he went back to the Arts Center after lunch. He and Bert, his housemate, always came home for lunch. Lucy had once summed up the household for somebody, "They have His and His towels."

They had no such thing. Seen together, Bert and Alec gave off that pleasant if rather humdrum feeling of Old Marrieds. Bert did the marketing and cooking and tended the vegetable garden. Alec collected old jazz records and played the piano rather well. He often played for Bert after dinner. Lucy herself had no special craving for Dixieland jazz; in the way of light music she preferred old musical-comedy tunes, and Alec, who was always doing thoughtful things for friends, had dug up a lot of tattered sheet music in New York, in a store on Fourth Avenue, so that he could play nostalgic favorites for her from Anything Goes, Showboat, Sweet Adeline, Babes in Arms . . . all the shows Lucy and Hal had gone to when they were young illustrators, in love with themselves and New York.

Alec answered the phone on the fifth ring, sounding breathless and rushed. A curt "Yes?" instead of "Hello." But when he heard Lucy's voice, her plaintive, "You sound so damn brisk," he changed to his easiest, most affectionate tone. "Never, with you. Not brisk, brusque, brask—that's a good word, brask—I will say it but not sound it. The dogsbody of the Dilworth Arts Center presents his compliments to the beauteous lady. . . ." Sometimes his nonsense talk got a bit thick, but he always shifted before it became really cloying and said things, with genuine sweetness, that a listener needed to hear. "I changed your three water colors to a better spot in the gallery this morning. They're even more marvelous than I'd thought."

Lucy, who thought the same thing was greedy for a second helping of praise, and for company. "Stop in on your way back to town. I want to talk to you before the meeting."

"I have one foot in the car. Be there in three minutes."

And he was. As his shiny little black Japanese bug came scurrying up the driveway, Lucy noted with satisfaction that Inspector McDougal had left off his mothball-burying to stand up and look over to see who was coming. Alec waved cheerily. The inspector made an unenthusiastic flip of his trowel.

This may have made Lucy's own greeting even more animated. She hurried out to the car, her small, vivid face radiating pleasure, and tucked her arm through Alec's to lead him back to the terrace. He was only a few inches taller than her own five feet one.

Alec presented her with a jar of preserves. "Homemade raspberry jam. It's really special stuff. Bert made it last weekend." He didn't sound in the least coy; he sounded like a husband who is pleased and proud of his wife's talents. And he reacted to Lucy's new summer suit in the same direct way. "*Very* good. If Grace had your clothes sense. . . . I'm awfully fond of her—you know that—but I wish somebody could slip-cover her or something, to soften the edges. I mustn't stay more than six minutes."

He perched on the edge of a chaise, looking, as always, trim and freshly scrubbed, like a well-fed, overage choirboy. His milk-chocolate-brown hair fitted his head like a helmet. His gray denim jacket and darker gray slacks were beautifully tailored, his tie was wide but not wild. He was thirty years younger than Lucy, and, unlike her, he was apt to tell his age frankly, or pat his rounding paunch and complain that he'd have to take up bicycling again.

He had a smile that curved up like a half moon in his rather round face. "If you lured me here to find out what I think of Grace's new man—I haven't met him yet."

This made Lucy feel better. "Neither have I. Grace is playing him close to her chest."

Alec laughed appreciatively, a good "Ho-ho-ho" that cheered Lucy even more. She revived like a flower that's been watered. Her large, dark blue, still beautiful eyes sparkled. "I'm so glad you came. Tell me, what's this meeting about? Your assistant just said Grace had asked that we come if we possibly could. Is Grace going to exhibit her catch to the board members? 'What I Did with My Summer Vacation' or 'Among the Interesting Souvenirs of My Trip'?"

Rather to her annoyance, Alec didn't laugh again. He looked glum, and for the first time she noticed he was getting a bit jowly. "I wasn't let in on the secret. I was in New York the last few days, anyway. But Martha said Grace and her boyfriend spent hours at the Center yesterday, and they were using my office between forays. Martha filled me in this morning. 'Miss Dilworth's friend looks like a movie star but not the sort who rides motorcycles and kills people.'" Alec mimicked his assistant's curlicued voice: "'His name is Davin Lowry, which I think is such an interesting name.' He told her he'd been connected with a sculpture museum on the West Coast. So maybe Grace is planning to boot me out and give him my job."

Alec said it lightly, mockingly, but Lucy wasn't fooled. And if she demanded a lot from her friends, she usually gave lavishly in return, with spirit and affection. "Just let her try it. All the members of the board would rise up in a body and screech at her."

"And then present me with a set of matched luggage for conscientious servitude, on retirement. After all, they don't have too much say about hiring and firing. It *is* the Dilworth Arts and Crafts Center, and Grace owns ninety-two percent of the stock."

"She'd never be fool enough to let you go. God, when I think of the artsy-craftsy female who used to run the place. . . ."

"Well, we still have the hobbyhorse crafts. But I can't line all the amateurs up against a wall and shoot them."

"I suppose not." Lucy sounded regretful. "At least you've managed to bring in some really good things." It wasn't modesty that kept her from adding, "Including my paintings." She considered that too obvious to mention.

Alec had lifted a ceramic ashtray and turned it over to look at the signature. "Nice. Sometimes I think if I see one more ceramic salt shaker shaped like a toadstool, I'll twitch. Last year, owls were big. Everybody in the ceramics class was turning out owls—to-wit-to-woo. Some unconscious yearning for wisdom, no

6

doubt. Silly but touching. But toadstools are too utterly nauseating. I'm sure it's a symptom of the poisonous world we live in."

This was so unlike Alec that Lucy felt alarmed. "Why don't you tiptoe in some night with an ax and smash the whole lot? It would do you good."

Alec smiled faintly. "I promise not to quote you at the board meeting this afternoon. Now that Daddy Dilworth has gone to his hellish reward, I may be able to hire a pro to teach some classes and raise the standards above toadstools—that is, if I still have the job. I must say, in all fairness, Grace has been awfully good to me."

"Good! Who else but you would work thirteen hours a day and humor the dabblers and the old ladies with crewel embroidery and—"

"Oh, crewel is out. The newest IN thing with old ladies is hand-painting china."

"Again! Shades of my Great-aunt Gertrude. She daubed violets all over the family's white Wedgwood."

"Did I tell you we had at least three hundred kids at the jazz-record concert last week? They were mad for Berrigan and Bix. But they were just as mad for the early Brubeck, and that depresses me. As for the piano recital tonight—it's a female who ripples Mozart like a spayed kitten on the keys."

Lucy looked bored, and he shifted at once to regain her interest. "Whatever happens, I'll put on one really smashing art show before the millennium. Don't forget the opening is two weeks from Saturday. I'm late sending out the notices because the mimeographing machine broke down. Bert fixed it last night."

"Will you two help me choose which of my water colors to put in?"

Alec said they'd be delighted. He went on in a swallowed-up voice, "Bert and I've never been so happy as we are here. I loathed California, especially after"—he stopped abruptly, then said too quickly, jumping the gap—"after the big earthquake. It isn't the shock—it's the aftershocks that really get you down." His beamish-boy look had sagged even more.

7

Something gave you the aftershocks, Lucy thought, and it wasn't the kind that shows up on a seismograph.

"Bert and I were going to have a housewarming next month after we finished laying the terrace. Now we'll be more apt to have a house-cooling. Sorry, I'm not exactly Pollyanna of Sunnybrook Farm today. I'm more in a mood to scatter worms on my head."

"Grace has no intention of firing you." Lucy could endow wishful thinking with the ring of authority. "And you said yourself her man is supposed to look like a movie star—not a curator."

"So did Thomas Hoving of the Metropolitan. We come in all shapes and sizes. Anyway, I'm more nanny than curator."

"That's what they need," Lucy said, with more truth than tact. "As long as they let the amateurs run loose."

"Martha Teague wants to give a course in weaving without a loom. All you use are your fingers." His plump white hands wiggled in the air, demonstrating. "Am I a warp or a woof?" As he brought down his arm, he glanced at the calendar wrist watch Bert had given him for his last birthday. It was self-winding, immersible, and kept quite good time, but Alec had complained it never seemed to know what day it was. "Good Lord! Two ten." He leaped up. "Time's winged chariot could run over me while I sit here at your feet."

It was perhaps unfortunate that Inspector McDougal came onto the terrace in time to catch the last sentence. The inspector was not a man to indulge in purple-nonsense talk. He looked hot and annoyed, as well he might after burying that many mothballs in the dirt, and his costume did nothing to lighten the effect: old khaki pants, a grayish sweat shirt and a visor cap stained with Bug-off mosquito repellent. Standing next to Alec, he looked much taller than his six feet three, and stalkier. (His height was one reason Lucy had first thought of pairing him off with Grace.) And next to the inspector, Alec looked like something out of an ultrasmart men's store display, slightly squashed.

Lucy, trying to link these disparate entities, held up her present. "Look, Mac, homemade raspberry jam. I'm going to get the recipe."

8

This was cleverer, or at least less babble-mouth, than it sounded. For a bony man, Inspector McDougal was incongruously interested in food. But at the moment he gave the impression that he could think of better uses for a raspberry.

Alec, hypersensitive to emanations, said quickly he was just leaving. "Ta-ta." It was one of his sillier phrases. "See you at the meeting."

As he walked to his car with brisk, short steps, his rear end bounced just a bit. Lucy, watching the inspector watching this, was rather annoyed. At Alec for bouncing, and at the inspector for noticing. "You shouldn't be so narrow-minded. What have you against homosexuals?"

Her tenant had stretched out on the chaise Alec had just vacated, with his sneakered feet dangling over the edge. "Nothing. But I wouldn't want my sister to marry one."

The inspector so seldom made jokes that Lucy was surprised into laughing, and then felt disloyal. "Seriously, it's an attitude that appalls me, in somebody in your field. As if it's criminal to be queer."

The inspector, who was lighting a cigarette, flung down the match as if he'd been burned. "It has never had the slightest effect on my professional judgment. And I never let my men bait homos."

"But I keep reading in the papers about plain-clothes men loitering in men's rooms till some poor devil makes a pass. Like Oscar Wilde."

"It was the prosecution's lawyer who pinned Wilde. Sometimes I think that's why England has been so far ahead of us in passing the Sexual Offences Act—to make up for what they did to Wilde. 'Between consenting adults' is long overdue here. Only five states have got rid of the old sodomy laws."

"I always think of sodomy as something you do with a swan. But there was a boy near Wingate who did it with a goat. The farmer had him arrested, so the police told the boy he could either go to jail or enlist in the army, and he enlisted and was killed in the Second World War. That didn't seem fair, and anyway, it was a female goat."

9

"Well, if he'd been arrested in a men's room at least he wouldn't have been sent into the army. But homos still live in a weird state of limbo, and I'm all for some new laws that give them a decent break."

"You may think that way professionally, but you don't act it socially. Every time Alec comes around, you look as if you'd like to kick him in the crotch."

The inspector gave a short bark of laughter. He was a fair-enough-minded man to know Lucy had a point. He was also self-analytical enough to know she was right for the wrong reasons. He had been her tenant for almost a year living in what had been her husband's studio behind the house. And more than any other person, Lucy, in her astringent way, had been responsible for helping him glue the pieces of his self-respect back together. But the structure was still precarious enough so that it needed bolstering daily. He had liked having a man-around-the-place role. He had felt needed, and nourished by friendship. Also by Lucy's dinners. One of her stipulations for renting the studio was that her tenant would be a guinea pig when she tried out new dishes. It had not been a hardship. Until Alec and Bert had moved into a little house down the road early that spring, the inspector had been sole guest and head of the table at many a dinner. In return, he provided all the liquor, shoveled snow, tended the garden (a labor of love mixed with curses at Mother Nature), and slapped Lucy down whenever she tried to get bossy. Now Alec and Bert were slicing into his claim, or nibbling it away. Alec, especially, seemed to pop in and out at all hours, bringing some fool piece of old sheet music—kitchy-kitchy-koo stuff—asking Lucy's advice on wallpaper and curtains, and taking her off on pointless expeditions from which she returned tired and entirely too happy.

Lucy, who often rode her intuition like a broomstick, said, "Alec and Bert make a fuss over me and take me places. Even at my age, I feel moldy if I have to go out in the evening with a woman." The very thought of it made her push up her curly white hair till it stood on end. "I want a man for an escort, or at least a reasonable facsimile. And homos are often more fun than women. Alec doesn't open up with you, but he's really a very amusing man even when he's depressed. He said today he felt like scattering worms on his head." She laughed rather more than necessary, like a young girl convulsing herself.

The inspector looked at her stonily. "If that's your idea of wit. . . ."

This stung Lucy into snapping, "I don't find your wooden-Indian act very gay either."

"I never said Alec and Bert weren't *gay*," McDougal said, with unworthy emphasis.

It made Lucy even madder. "At least they appreciate me and they say so. You never say so. It's no wonder that your—" She broke off, looking guilty.

—"that my wife left me for a man who plied her with appreciation." He sat staring out at the thick green lawn he'd fed so faithfully that spring. Moles had made a new hump of upheaval near the terrace, but he wasn't seeing it now; he was staring painfully at the wreckage of his marriage. Eileen had had such childlike enthusiasms, a new one every week or month. She'd been so rushingly eager to reach out her pretty arms and embrace anything from Zen Buddhism to massive doses of Vitamin C as a cure-all. If he'd tried to share her excitements—but it had all seemed so naïvely silly. If he'd encouraged her more, tried to enjoy the prism flashes of each new fad that caught her ardent interest. . . . The trouble was that a cop had no time for the prism flashes; he couldn't go flittering off down the side paths into escapism. But other cops had managed to keep their wives happy, or at least to keep them. . . .

Lucy, watching his face lengthen into what she privately thought of as his Rouault-on-the-Cross expression, was horrified at what she'd done. "Mac, I'm an idiot. I didn't mean it at all. You know how things spurt off the top of my head before I hear what I'm thinking. I don't even think that. You're worth a hundred of that third-rate director she married."

"He's not third-rate," the inspector said perversely. "Eileen never went in for the third-rate. Her new husband is considered very talented."

"Don't be so bloody chivalrous. He sounds to me like the sort who thinks if something has form and meaning it's not art. 'Only chaos is genius.' I've had a bellyful of that sort."

So had the inspector, but he still felt a stubborn need to lend armor to the enemy. "You've never met him. He's very good-looking. Women fall all over him."

"More fools they. I feel sorry for your wife."

"My ex-wife," McDougal said somberly.

"I think you ought to get married again."

A year ago, this remark would have turned McDougal to ice or made him erupt. But now he was enough recovered, and enough used to Lucy, to say politely, "Whom did you have in mind? At least, you might give me advance notice, so I can fold my tent and scram."

Lucy waved toward the house next door, which was five times the size of her own. "Grace Dilworth came home this week. The only reason you haven't met her before is that she was staying in New York all the time her father was in the hospital, and then after he died she went off on a long trip. She had a father fixation, and—"

"And that's why you thought she might settle for me?"

"Come off it. You're a very attractive man, but you're still too sunk into yourself. You didn't just retire from your job. You tried to retire from life."

"I retired from marriage—or was forcibly retired. And nothing could persuade me to try it again. So forget it. You're not going to sacrifice me on the altar."

"It's too late for Grace, anyway," Lucy said, with regret. "If it weren't, I wouldn't have told you. She brought home a man of her own."

The inspector looked amused. "Bully for Grace. That'll teach you. The last time you tried to matchmake somebody, you picked a murderer."

"Well, except for that, it would have been a very good match. And if you ever involve me in another murder among friends, it will be over my dead body."

"I'd prefer you to take a more active role," the inspector said courteously.

"You never told me how much help I was the last time."

"I never told you how much you obstructed me, either."

The air around Lucy crackled. Her temper tantrums were usually as brief as a summer storm, but while they lasted, the thunderbolts hurled at random were enough to drive strong men under the table. The inspector, an imaginative man, had no desire to provoke any such outburst, and he could be diplomatic when he thought it feasible. He now thought it feasible. "I almost forgot —Sergeant Terrizi wants you to come to his and Angie's engagement party."

Lucy was instantly diverted. She adored parties. And she was fond of Sergeant Terrizi, who had been her yard boy for years. Nicky Terrizi had been fourteen years old when he first came to work, with dangling, dirty hands and miraculously green thumbs. "I'd love to. When?"

"Two weeks from Saturday night."

"Oh, hell! That's the night the show opens at the Dilworth Center. And I have to be there. I'm on the committee. Why don't you come to the opening with me and then we'll go on to Nicky's party afterward?"

"Not me."

So the storm broke anyway. One of the milder things Lucy said was that she could understand why the police were called pigs. "You're a selfish introvert pig."

By the time she had driven halfway into Wingate, three miles away, she was planning a special dinner for her tenant as atonement. If the meeting didn't last long, maybe a beef bourguignon. Use the rest of the Rémy Martin in the sauce . . . pick up some more red wine . . . get a piece of salt pork to simmer with the beef. And wild rice instead of Uncle Ben's. No, wild rice was too insanely expensive; she didn't have to atone that extravagantly. Of course, she'd been bitchy, but if it jolted Mac out of his shell, it would do him good. He should get married to somebody who'd massage his ego and make him feel actively male again. Grace would have been good at that; she was like that girl in Chekhov's

"Darling." Whatever the man cared about would be what Grace cared about, with passionate intensity. Sam Dilworth had trained her that way from babyhood. And in Sam's own ruthless way, he had been shrewd about sizing up people; Grace ought to have enough of Sam in her to see that McDougal was no ordinary policeman. Maybe Grace's new man was only a passing-through fancy. Maybe he really *was* just a souvenir of the trip, brought home to show off, a perfectly understandable impulse.

A traffic light turning yellow roused her to step on the gas and spurt ahead. Lucy had never regarded a yellow light as cautionary; it was a come-on. She muttered a few minor curses because all the parking spaces within a half block of the Dilworth Center were taken. Or at least all the legitimate spaces. Why the hell didn't the Center buy that vacant lot behind the garden and turn it into a parking lot? Messy overgrown thing—not doing anybody any good as it was. Somehow this grievance gave her an excuse to nudge her snub-nosed little Saab into a spot seven feet from a fire hydrant. In her opinion, this gave everybody leeway to maneuver. She wouldn't have been too devastated if the Dilworth Center had a small fire, although preferably some other day, and just enough to damage the front of the building.

The Center was designed in the pseudo-New England tradition rampant in Wingate even unto the A & P: white pillars, fanlight doorway, fierce brass eagle flapping on top. Colonial graciousness crossbred with a look of "The big bird will getcha if you don't watch out."

A cobblestone path, a booby trap for high heels, meandered in from the sidewalk and led, eventually, to the front entrance. It was flanked by squared-off clumps of pachysandra, with a birdbath and forsythia bush to the left, and a sundial and Burford holly bush on the right, bordered by a box hedge so closely barbered it looked artificial.

The one really attractive spot was the rose garden in the rear, but even it had its hazards: steep, picturesque old stone steps went down to it, and once there, a scattering of rustic benches could leave splinters in the behinds of unwary sitters. But the roses were glorious, and at this time of year, in late June, they were at their loveliest.

Lucy, starting up the cobblestone path at a reckless pace, decided she'd go around and have a quick look from the top of the steps before the meeting.

"Hello, Lucy." The local architect responsible for perpetrating the Center and landscaping the grounds had popped out from behind the holly bush, smiling and extending his hand. (His most passionate gesture seemed to be shaking hands, in a well-bred way.) Apart from his lack of talent, or his weakmindedness in following Sam Dilworth's orders to the letter, Lucy had nothing against Fred Thorndike. In fact, she was mildly fond of him. He was a sandy little man, sandy hair and tweaky moustache, reddish sandy skin, sand-colored jackets, and always a waistcoat that went with his pipe and his Cambridge accent. The Thorndikes were a very old New England family, and Fred seemed more like an Englishman, a small county squire, than a Yankee. Looking at him, you might think Paul Revere had never gone horseback riding and that the British still held their most troublesome colonies.

At the moment, Fred sounded un-Britishly eager. "Have you seen Grace? The Farmingtons and I have a delightful surprise for her. I wanted to tell her before the meeting."

Lucy had once thought that Fred, a widower, teetered on the brink of being in love with Grace, but Grace was a half foot taller and had been surrounded by Sam Dilworth. She had gone riding and hunting with her father, played tennis and golf with him, even sat with him keeping score on bull versus bear at his private ticker tape. Sam had been the son of a coal miner and he'd escaped, early on, to make his millions. Fred was the blue-blood run thin; he had inherited some of his forebears' money but none of their sporting ways. He collected Audubon prints and was an assiduous bird watcher. And he'd been devoted to Sam, and seemingly content to trot trivially in Sam's giant shadow.

But with Sam dead and underground, Lucy thought Fred might be feeling taller and more adequate as a suitor. He was looking and sounding that way. She told him she hadn't seen Grace or her guest yet.

"Oh, does she have a guest? I'm glad. It will be good for her to have another girl around for companionship."

As everybody in Wingate but Fred Thorndike knew, Grace's guest was equipped with a penis. Lucy thought of saying, "It's a boy," but that seemed rather blunt. Fred was thin-skinned, and kindness made Lucy want to cushion the shock he was due for. "She brought home some art expert—a shipboard acquaintance— he's interested in sculptures."

"Splendid. I knew the trip would take her out of herself. In fact, I was the one who talked her into going. I hope he'll give a lecture at the Center while he's here."

Even to Lucy, the conversation was beginning to conjure up a picture of a spruce little gentleman with a Vandyke beard and polysyllabic jargon.

So there was a slightly cross-eyed split in her mind when she saw Grace coming up the walk with one of the handsomest young men Lucy had ever seen. A phrase from a Saul Bellow novel describing somebody's lover zipped through her head: "Tall, from California, marvelous teeth."

The man was at least three inches taller than Grace. And nobody would have to slip-cover Grace now, to soften her angular edges.

2

From the neck up, Grace had always been handsome: a strongly chiseled profile and well-set head, with glossy dark hair pulled back in the classic bun favored by Roman matrons and pioneer women. But the rest of her had had the slightly disjointed look of a two-legged colt dressed by Abercrombie & Fitch. Bulky suits, shirtwaist dresses implacably striped up and down, large, splendidly polished leather oxfords.

Lucy Ramsdale, surveying her now—the soft focus, all-of-a-piece look—thought, My God, what sex hath wrought. She had been ready to say tartly, "I can see why you've been too busy to have time for old friends," but she was deflected by the warmth of Grace's hug and her "We stopped to pick you up—I wanted to be sure you'd come to the meeting—but you'd already left."

Instead, she said, "Grace, you look wonderful. I love that dress."

"Davin helped me pick out some things on the ship. They had quite a good boutique." Quite good was an understatement.

"And she paid for them out of her filthy riches. And bought me a gold cigarette case which I'll pawn whenever I'm broke." He gave Lucy an amused look. *I beat you to it.*

"Davin! Stop trying to sound like an adventurer or something." And to Lucy, "He cares less about money than anyone I ever met. And he was horrified by the cigarette case. He made me take it back to the shop."

"So that we could buy something that cost even more."

"But that wasn't for you. You never want anything for yourself. Except the silver cup for the championship at deck tennis, on the ship. He beat even me to win it. He's terrific." She looked at him with the delight of a child on Christmas morning who'd never believed anything so wonderful would come down the chimney.

Seen close to, the man was even more attractive, because his face was lit by a quicksilver, restless intelligence. Lucy, with an artist's eye, noted the sensitively cut mouth, the lean-boned frame, the long head rising to the faintest suggestion of a faun's peak. . . .

The object of her survey said easily, "Grace has been so busy telling you my good points she hasn't introduced us. I'm Davin Lowry."

"So I'd heard. The grapevine in Wingate is so strong we swing on it from tree to tree, like monkeys."

The man gave a deep shout of laughter. "You live up to your reputation. Grace told me you were the liveliest member of the board."

"That wouldn't take much doing," Lucy said, looking meaningfully at several examples now clustered on the other side of the path. She was relieved that Fred Thorndike didn't seem shattered by his first glimpse of Grace's guest. He was talking earnestly to Myra and George Farmington.

"I thought Fred had already gone to East Hampton for the summer." Grace sounded dismayed; she'd reverted to an old, nervous mannerism of brushing one hand across her cheek like a colt twitching off a fly.

"He came back especially for this meeting. George Farmington called him."

"Oh." Bad cess to George, was what it sounded like to Lucy. She saw Fred look their way, but it was like him to be diffident about barging in. "Fred's very anxious to talk to you."

"The one person I absolutely must see before the meeting is Mario. You know, Davin, the gardener. He ought to be told ahead."

Instead of going around to the garden by the side path, which would have taken her past Fred and the Farmingtons, Grace simply stepped over a box hedge and bolted toward the back.

Davin Lowry gestured inconspicuously toward the others. "Fill me in, will you?" He made it sound like, You're the one whose opinion I trust. "Fred who?"

"Thorndike. His family came here when Tories were still socially acceptable. He's a local architect, and he's been crazy about Grace for years." Wouldn't hurt to let this man know Grace had other strings to her bow.

Davin nodded, filing it away. "And the other couple with him?"

"George and Myra Farmington. George is president of the bank, and he always seems to be rubbing his hands together genially as if he'd just finished counting the assets and was longing to loan them to deserving customers. But Hal and I applied for a loan when we were building a studio behind the house, and George dilated as if he didn't think artists were a safe risk. He and Myra are a perfect couple, because they deserve each other."

Myra Farmington, a handsomely lacquered woman fighting fifty, turned as if she sensed she were being talked about and waved in a gracious way. Lucy waved back.

"Myra married over her head and she takes her ancestors-in-law very seriously and worries away at their bones through the County Historical Society."

"I think I met the braided female here yesterday." He was looking at Alec's assistant, Martha Teague, who wore her hair in round-and-round braids like a hooked rug.

"Mrs. Teague. She teaches craft classes, and now she's taken up weaving without a loom. If Ophelia had had a hobby like that, she might have been sound as a nut."

Davin's deep, rolling laugh made her feel wonderfully, wittily feminine. "And the quivering creature talking to Mrs. Teague?"

It was an apt description of Flora Pollit, who quivered over Causes. Most recently, Flora had taken ecology to her widowed bosom with such fervor she had exhorted Lucy in the supermarket not to buy any detergents and had announced she was even making her own soap, to which Lucy had snapped, "Of human blubber, no doubt."

Lucy was still exasperated because Flora had campaigned, successfully, to keep the township from spraying trees against cankerworms, gypsy moths, and other hideous despoilers. As a result, at least half the trees around Wingate were denuded, and worms dropped like anti-manna. "Mario Sandini, the gardener, had to sneak in here at night to spray his roses when Flora wasn't looking. They're the love of his life."

Davin said quickly, "The garden is going to be handsomer than ever when Grace gets through with—"

Lucy's attention was deflected because Alec had come to the door and motioned urgently to George Farmington. As the two men vanished inside, Davin said, "Who's that?"

"Alec Foster. A friend of mine who runs this place. It's a thankless job, with amateurs crawling out of the woodwork all wanting to do things with their hands. But he's still managed to get some good professional things in here. I hope you don't think you're going to replace him."

"As the head keeper of a bunch of amateurs?" Davin's dark eyebrows shot up. "God forbid. I'd go dotty."

It was not only a gratifying answer, but a sensible one. Lucy gave him a dazzling smile of approval, and a pat on the arm. "I think I'm going to like you."

Davin, who was almost a foot taller, bent down with the manly-protector air Lucy often evoked. "I want you to. And not just because something tells me"—he glanced at the brass eagle flapping above the door, and added lightly—"let's say, a big bird told me the rest of the board may not approve of my—" He broke off as Myra Farmington and Flora Pollit closed in, palpably determined to meet the star turn.

Lucy never lingered long in a group in which somebody else had the spotlight. Besides, she wanted to find Alec.

As she went up the path, Mario Sandini came around the side of the building, pushing a wheelbarrow which he dropped abruptly and kicked, with a Sicilian-bandit kind of scowl. This was so unlike the exuberant Mario that Lucy stopped, waiting for him to notice her. Mario was one of her most articulate admirers in Wingate; looking at her white hair, he'd said once, "There's fire under that snow." Whenever she went to his nursery, he would choose one of his most magnificent roses and present it, with a Gallic flourish, for her to pin on her dress.

"Mario, I hear your niece and Sergeant Terrizi are having their engagement party soon."

The bandit scowl was superseded by a beaming, avuncular air. Mario came toward her with the purposeful lope that often reminded Lucy of Harpo chasing a blonde in old Marx Brothers movies. Sandini had never pinched her behind, but over the years he'd often looked as if he'd like to; the older one got, the more gratifying that was. And in a swarthy, muscular way, he was quite good-looking.

"Signora Ramsdale! I would hardly have known you—you look so young. You'll be at the party? That Angie! Would you believe it—when she was sixteen she wanted to be a nun. What a waste, eh?"

Lucy agreed. Sergeant Terrizi's Angie was a distractingly pretty girl. "Poor priests. They'd have had to spend all day in a cold shower, mumbling their chastity vows."

Mario, in his enjoyment over this sally, displayed a wealth of gold fillings. He pushed his old felt work hat back on his head, the better to converse. "She got a good boy in Nicky. But a cop isn't so safe as a husband these days—more like a duck in a shooting gallery. He shoulda stayed in my greenhouse. I'd have made him a partner."

"He was the best gardener I ever knew—except you, of course. And you trained him. By the way, Mario"—she tried to remember just what Davin had said—"I hear your garden is going to be bigger and better than ever."

Sandini reacted as if she'd jabbed him with a spading fork. He scowled at her, spat on a dainty clump of moss, and took off.

Lucy was so put out by this rudeness that she sat down shakily on a bench just inside the lobby. How dared he? I'll never buy anything from his damn nursery again. . . . She could hear her husband's quiet voice: "Lucy, you have to stop trying to make

21

everybody behave exactly as you think they should behave. If they get out of line, don't flounce around being indignant. They have their reasons, or un-reasons. And a lot of the time it has nothing whatever to do with you."

In her head, she had known Hal was right, although she had once told him furiously he sounded like a cliché psychologist, and he'd said, "You can't bear to think most clichés got to be clichés because they're true."

We were like Jack Spratt and his wife. I thought loose, Hal thought lean—I'm off balance without him. I'm getting to be a mean, selfish old woman.

The word "old" was an astringent enough expletive to produce an instant reflex. She opened her handbag, got out her compact, decided her pretty nose didn't need powder, fluffed her curly white hair, and went off at a fast clip. Find Alec and cheer him up.

But Alec's small, neat office, right off the lobby, was empty. As she came out, fuming, she was looking straight at the life-size portrait of Sam Dilworth that dominated, in fact, subjugated, the far wall. It was at least five feet across and seven feet deep, but Sam seemed to fill every inch of the canvas right up to the ornate gold frame. A mistake to paint a man full length, fully clothed, unless you were a Velasquez or Goya. This artist hadn't been a Velasquez or Goya; he had been a competent portrait painter, a minor friend of Hal's and Lucy's, and she remembered he'd had to do over the eyes and the jaw five or six times. He ranted to them, "Tinkering with the eyes, yes, that's standard, but what's so special about a jaw? I'd like to tell him to take his jawbone and shove it. . . ." The artist was paying alimony to four ex-wives at the time, so he had not told Sam Dilworth to take his jawbone and shove it. A year or so later, he had married a wealthy widow on Long Island, perhaps to keep from being a retoucher to any more tycoons like Sam.

Was that why Davin Lowry had latched onto Grace, as protection from Philistines? There was nothing like money to protect one from Philistines. But it was a hell of a reason for getting married.

The jaw in Sam's portrait seemed to have grown. It isn't the eyes that follow me around, it's the jaw. She had a slightly guilty feeling that her old adversary and neighbor would have expected more from her. *The guy wouldn't accept the gold cigarette case because he was after bigger game. You don't shoot a grasshopper when you're tracking a lion. You know that as well as I do, Lucy.*

I can't meddle in this, she told herself, or the portrait, virtuously. But as she went off, her conscience nagged like a pebble in a shoe.

3

She found Alec with George Farmington in the Mural Room, where meetings were joined, often with more heat than compatibility. The "murals" consisted of four hugely blown-up photographs of the country around Wingate—"Spring," "Summer," "Fall," "Winter." George Farmington had taken the pictures; photography was his alternate hobby to golf, and he took it almost as seriously. Right now, a projection screen blanketed the icicled beauty of "Winter." Lucy had long since stopped thinking of snow as beautiful. ("Another damn winter wonderland.") She hated winter, but she detested home movies even more. And the screen plus the projector the two men were diddling with spelled anathema. "God! Don't tell me Grace and her friend hauled us in here to show pictures of their trip. I'm damned if I'll be a captive audience."

George, an inexorable show-er of his own travel pictures, cleared his throat. He was tall and bald-domed, with a dignified bulge, and he gave the impression of rocking smoothly back and forth on his heels. "Now, Lucy, some of us enjoy that sort of thing. Nothing captive about it."

"People certainly enjoyed yours, George." Alec, scattering tact. "I hope you'll give us an illustrated talk on your trip to Greece."

George's rather florid cheeks swelled out in gratification. "Greatest trip we ever had. And I think, if I may say so, I was lucky enough to get some quite unusual pictures in Greece."

"Did you get any shots of the political prisoners being tortured?" Lucy asked in her deadliest sweet voice. Alec gave her a harried look, and she said, "I'm sorry. I'm in a foul temper. I thought this was going to be an amusing meeting, to show off Grace's guest and—"

"Fred Thorndike was telling us he's a well-known art expert," George put in.

Lucy said absently, "Oh, really?" before she remembered where Fred had got his information, or misinformation. "Anyway, if this meeting is just to show colored slides of every port on the cruise circuit—" She shrugged and made a half move back toward the door.

Alec pulled out one of the green vinyl armchairs grouped around the room. "You know very well you have no intention of missing the fireworks, so sit down and stop churning the air."

Lucy laughed and sat down, and remembered why she'd wanted to see Alec. "About that problem we were discussing, it's all settled. You needn't worry any more. I got it straight from the—er—stallion's mouth."

Alec's beamish-boy look returned. "You're beautiful. I think I'll make a phone call—just take a second."

He went hurrying off. Lucy was sure he'd gone to call Bert at Way Back Antiques, where Bert sold things, mostly to summer visitors, in a deprecating, gentlemanly way. When she thought of the reassurance she'd been able to give her two nice friends about their safe future in Wingate, she felt rather beamish herself, until she noticed it was almost three thirty. "George, why don't you round up the others? It's late as hell and I have to market for dinner."

George, who was lining up a box of slides with mathematical precision beside the projector, went off obediently.

"May I sit beside you for moral support?" Davin sat down as if he took the answer for granted.

"I'm not sure 'moral' is the kind of support you want." Lucy's tone was light, but she was looking at him intently as she said it.

Davin didn't try to evade her eyes or the implied question. He said in a low voice, "If you mean, Am I after Grace's money—no.

25

If I had been, I'd have married her before we came back to Wingate. Because I knew what her friends here would think—what you're thinking now. Young man on the make—heiress left all alone in the world."

"Do you realize she's never met anybody like you?"

To her surprise, he looked troubled, and disarmingly young. "I know. But what you don't realize is I'd never met a woman like her, either. She's so incredibly grateful and responsive. It's been a—a really tremendous thing for me, to help her change. It's made me feel, well—stronger than I ever felt in my life. If I said I didn't care about her money, I'd be a liar, but I don't want it for myself. I want to help her enjoy it in a way she never did before, for whatever time we're together."

"Grace doesn't strike me as a half-measures sort. Does she know this is temporary?"

"That's not what I said." He hesitated. "I can tell you one thing —I care more about Grace than any woman ever."

"I don't mean to pry—yes, I suppose I do. I'm an interfering old woman."

She waited to be contradicted, and Davin came in on cue.

"If you were an interfering old woman, I wouldn't have said a word. You're the sort who'll never be old. And you're entirely too perceptive. I don't know when I've talked like this to someone I've just met. And it's not because you 'remind me of my mother.' She was the original daughter of Dracula. It took me a long time to pull free, and even now I'm not sure. . . ."

Voices chattered in the corridor as he burst out, "I wish you *had* been my mother, damn it."

The look he gave her was so unmaudlin, so half-humorous, half-rueful, that she felt a spurt of affection. "If you ever feel like talking things over, I'll be your eccentric aunt next door." She patted his lean, tanned hand. "I mean that."

The gesture didn't escape Martha Teague, who had just come in. Martha's round eyes, behind horn rims, got even rounder, and she hurriedly veered away from their twosome to a group of empty chairs across the room.

Probably thinks I'm cradle-snatching. Maybe it's all to the good

26

if he and Grace don't get married. At least he's broken the ice—and you can't be a virgin twice, thank God. Now that Grace is lubricated, she'll be even better for McDougal. If the affair with Davin cools off. . . .

Davin was staring at "Spring" but not seeing it. In profile, with his mop of dark curls, he reminded her of a head of a Greek youth by Praxiteles. She was glad she'd never fallen in love with a wildly handsome man, although she could see how weaker-minded women might. Not that Grace was weak-minded. Unworldly, yes, but with enough of Sam Dilworth in her to resist being manipulated for long. Looking at Grace as she walked toward them, with a free, long stride, Lucy thought, she's leaped the fence. She's taking the hurdles Sam never let her try, and she's shaping up well.

"She's striking, isn't she?" Davin sounded quite fatuous. "You should have seen her the night of the captain's dinner. She was wearing a very simple white crepe—Givenchy—"

"What could be simpler than Givenchy?"

He laughed. "Oh, I know—but the thing is, she did something for the dress. She made other women look fluffy."

As Grace came up to them, he said, "I was just telling Mrs. Ramsdale how you knocked them cold the night of the captain's dinner."

"Oh, you! You're just prejudiced." It would have been unbearably roguish if it hadn't been so radiantly adoring. "Anyway, Lucy, he deserves all the credit. He picked out the dress and—oh, there's Alec." She waved.

"Grace! Welcome home. You look great." He almost stood on tiptoe to peck her cheek.

Davin jumped up and the two men shook hands in that brisk, gung-ho fashion that always amused Lucy. It was all so amiable, as they exchanged small talk—the How-do-you-like-Wingate—I-like-it-very-much variety—that Lucy's flash impression of two dogs sniffing each other warily seemed ridiculous.

Fred Thorndike came in and was determinedly jolly-friendly. "George tells me you're going to show some pictures today. Fine,

fine. I hope you'll have time to give us a longer talk on art while you're here."

He went on in that fashion; Lucy wasn't sure whether he was still being obtuse, or whether he'd finally realized the situation and felt it was only cricket to be gracious to a rival. She rather thought the latter.

"Grace, do you mind if I make a little announcement before we start? Myra and George and I have been cooking up a surprise for you."

Grace, with the careless kindness of somebody wrapped in her own happiness, said, "What fun, Fred. But we have a lot to cover today, so don't take too long."

Lucy, sitting between Grace and Davin, called to Alec, "Do sit down here with us so we can get started." She was so used to Alec humoring her that she was puzzled and hurt when he went over and joined his assistant, Martha Teague, and Flora Pollit. After the trouble she had gone to, making sure his job wasn't in jeopardy—Lucy thought it was really unpleasant of Alec. She saw Flora stick her doughy face within an inch of his nose and start a harangue, with gestures. Probably urging him to surrender his flit-gun. The Farmingtons and Fred Thorndike settled themselves in chairs directly in front of Alec, and when George, as chairman, got up to call the meeting to order, Myra watched him with the sleek pride of a helpmeet who always knows exactly what her husband will say and approves every word.

"Folks—" (Lucy wrinkled her nose fastidiously; she detested the word. Davin, on her left, noticed and murmured in her ear, "Yes, but 'artistic' is worse.")

". . . appreciate your coming here on short notice. I know several of you had other work to do, and we can't all be lucky enough to keep bankers' hours, ha-ha." Myra, who must have heard the joke only a few dozen times before, laughed extensively, although without showing her teeth. One or two of the others made polite sounds. Lucy yawned and began to revise her dinner menu. Pick up a chicken at Coleman's . . . make dumplings . . . and for a first course, the anchovy-and-onion tarts. . . .

". . . know you're as happy as I am to have our Grace back, and I think this is a fitting occasion to spring a little welcome-home surprise we've been planning. I don't want to take up any more of your time because I understand our guest, Mr. Lowry, has some beautiful pictures to show us later, and I'm sure we're in for an artistic treat." Davin nudged Lucy on "artistic." "So I'll call on Fred Thorndike because he's really the one who thought of this project in the first place, and I'm happy Myra and I could contribute our own small share." Whatever the Farmingtons were contributing, George obviously didn't think it was small. He gave off waves of self-satisfaction like a strong men's cologne. "Fred, will you take over?"

Fred got up, thrust his hands into the pockets of his jacket, and glanced quickly at Grace, with a shy, sweet smile. "This is by way of being a memorial to Sam Dilworth. It's something he wanted, and something the Center will benefit by. As we all know, he financed the building of the Center because he cared about Wingate. . . ."

Lucy thought, Sam built it as his own Sphinx and made sure his name was plastered right across the front.

". . . put in a modern parking lot right behind the rose garden with space for two hundred cars . . . system of electric conduits beneath the concrete to melt snow in winter. . . ."

Lucy missed the next part because Davin slammed his foot down with such vehemence it reverberated inside her, while Grace, on her right, whimpered, "Oh, no."

Fred was still talking. ". . . want to make it clear my part in this is very modest indeed, compared to Myra and George Farmington's. They are generously underwriting the entire cost of the project. As a first step, they'll buy the vacant lot behind the Center as soon as Grace and the other members of the board give us the go-ahead. Thank you." He sat down.

Grace leaned forward as if she were going to speak, then froze as if she wasn't quite sure what to say. Several people were clapping as Martha Teague popped up: "That's the dandiest idea I've heard of in ages. So many people have told me they'd just love to come to the Center oftener—for craft classes and concerts and things—but they can't ever find a place to park. I want to say I think the Farmingtons and Fred deserve a big vote of thanks."

Alec said he seconded that.

Davin was looking stonily straight ahead, and a muscle in his cheek jerked. Lucy noticed it with distaste. She didn't approve of other people having temper tantrums. Anyway, the parking lot was such a sensible idea she couldn't understand why anybody would be against it. Myra was looking over at Grace expectantly, but Grace was too concerned with Davin, trying to get his attention.

Flora Pollit sprang into the vacuum. "As the only one here who seems concerned with pollution, I want to point out that if we planted several hundred trees in that lot and made a little park, we'd be contributing far more to the well-being of every person who comes to the Center by countering the effects of carbon monoxide. It now takes *twenty* trees to enable each person to *breathe*—each man, woman, and child, although I believe a man needs more trees than a child because of larger lungs and longer exposure to poisonous air"—she managed to draw a breath herself—"anyway, it now averages out at twenty trees per person, because of the fumes from cars. So a parking lot would only increase this terrible pollution. Let people walk, as our forefathers did, on their own two feet."

Alec said soothingly, "Parked cars wouldn't emit carbon monoxide, Flora."

"But they would the minute they moved. And they have to move sometime. They can't just sit there."

This seemed a fairly unarguable premise. Alec looked over at Grace for support, but Grace still was oblivious to anybody but Davin. Lucy poked her. "Say something."

As Grace got up, she reverted again to the old mannerism of brushing her hand across her cheek. "It's dear and generous and thoughtful of all three of you. . . ."

Myra and George were smiling complacently, benefactors caught in the act. Fred Thorndike looked shyly pleased.

"But I'm afraid it's impossible, because we already have other

30

plans. I bought that vacant lot myself this morning. I mean, Davin and I did."

Fred Thorndike took out his pipe and clenched it, unlit, between his teeth.

"We're going to have a garden for modern sculpture that will include both the lot and what is now the rose garden, and it's going to be very exciting. But Davin Lowry can explain that much better than I can. Will you, Davin?"

Davin turned on his most charming smile. "I'll try. But one of the many nice things about Grace is that she comes right to the point, and she's already given you the gist of the whole idea. All I can do is fill in some details. Miss Pollit, I'll start out by saying I can promise you our sculpture won't give off any poisonous fumes."

Flora Pollit beamed so fulsomely she looked as if she were melting like grease. She was a minority of one. The rest of the group on that side of the room were so obviously dubious, even dismayed, that Davin abandoned all attempts at cosiness. His tone became cooler, and a shade arrogant. "It's obvious that whoever landscaped this place originally was going on the quaint theory that 'the balance of composition consists of evenly inverted repetition on each side of the vertical axis.' A birdbath to balance a sundial, and a rose arbor to balance two benches, a lilac bush, etcetera ad moribundum. . . ."

Lucy, who thought Fred was already having a rough enough time, kicked Davin in the shin, as a hint to lay off that subject. Either she didn't kick hard enough or Davin was too wound up to notice.

"It was the bland old theory that the attention must flow from object to object without startling the eye of the beholder. But we *want* to startle—to surprise—even to shock. And from what Grace has told me of her father, that's the way he himself operated—boldly, no pussyfooting, doing the unexpected and bringing it off every time. When Grace showed me that portrait in the lobby, I could imagine Sam Dilworth putting over a sensational deal and saying to an aide, 'Let's see what the competition thinks of *that*.' He was ahead of whatever trend was current, in business,

31

and that's what we aim to do here—to create the unexpected in the midst of Colonial architecture. And I think Sam Dilworth would have enjoyed the galvanic impact of our sculpture garden. People will notice it because they won't be able to help it. They'll be stabbed in the eye and transfixed. . . ."

Grace cut in, "Davin, if you'd show them a few slides, I'm sure they'd get a clearer idea. Alec, would you run the projector, and Davin will comment on the various pieces. Do you want the lights turned off, Davin?"

"Not necessary. We have a special film. But of course if anybody would prefer cover of darkness so he can bash me over the head. . . ."

Lucy said, "Better not take any chances. And let's get on with the show."

Grace, returning to her seat, passed him on his way to the projector and gave him so loving a look it reminded Lucy, incongruously, of a little girl licking a lollipop. "You're quite right, Mrs. Ramsdale. I lack Grace's gift of brevity."

"Foster, let's have the first slide—ah, yes, 'Moon God.' "

"Moon God" was a huge lump of iron, vaguely circular, hollowed inside, and the outer rim edged all around with sharp spikes perhaps ten inches long, nostalgically reminiscent of the Spanish Inquisition's torture rack.

"Strong and cruel and exciting," Davin said. "Like life today. We've gotten away from Moore's earth-mother curves—figures so whitely wholesome they might have been carved out of Ivory Soap. And the same for Maillol's nudes, those endless bland buttocks which if laid end to end would discourage even a sex maniac."

The expressions on the faces of his audience might have discouraged more than a sex maniac. He's lost even Flora Pollit, Lucy thought, looking across the room: she'd settle for carbon monoxide. George Farmington's face was a mottled mauve; Myra's back was rigidly arched; Martha Teague looked as if she'd been attacked by a friend with a can opener. Fred Thorndike was staring at the floor.

"I happened to know the sculptor was having a show open in

New York about the time our ship docked. So Grace and I were lucky enough to grab 'Moon God' right then for our garden."

Martha Teague said, "But children would hurt themselves on that thing." Her round, wholesome face, under the braided rug of hair, was anxious.

"We aren't planning this sculpture garden for children. Perhaps juveniles and amateurs have already been given too much preference around here."

Lucy, who had often said the same thing in private, was perversely annoyed at Davin; he was going out of his way to be unpleasant.

Davin clicked his fingers. "Next."

Nothing happened. Alec's polite smile had congealed into sullenness.

"*Next,* Foster."

Alec was taking his time about pressing the ejector.

Grace fidgeted in her chair. Lucy murmured, "You'll have to keep Mario's roses." She wanted to add, "And Alec's job," but Alec was being so uncooperative she knew this wasn't the moment.

Grace didn't bother to keep her voice down. "I've already told Mario. It's all settled. The workmen are starting tomorrow, and they'll clear out the arbor first thing, so we can see where we want to place things."

Lucy made a face. "Davin could at least use some tact."

Grace smiled, then said very softly, "He's so honest and direct —he's like Sam. He'll step on some toes, but he'll get things done. And I'll back him all the way, even if—"

Alec had got the next slide into focus.

"Thank you so much." Davin's tone grated with sarcasm. "And right side up, too."

Alec said coolly, "If it makes any difference."

"To people who know art—yes."

Lucy, who knew art and knew what she didn't like (which was plenty), stared at the large white oblong shape, upended; it was pinched in at the lower end so that the whole thing seemed top-heavy, like a monolith walking on its head.

33

"'Lot's Wife Looking at Civilization,'" Davin announced. "This marble came from the quarry near Positano, and the Italian sculptor is already in the Museum of Modern Art."

Fred Thorndike said, "Locked in a closet?" which, for Fred, was quite a riposte.

Lucy saw Myra half rise as if she were ready to walk out, but George pulled her down and muttered to her. Probably reminding her Grace is a big depositor, and he gets a fat fee for being executor of Sam's estate. George looked so deflated, and so old, suddenly, that Lucy felt rather sorry for him. It was nice of him to want to pay for a parking lot, she thought, and we need that a damn sight more than a sculpture garden . . . but I can't vote on his side. Most of the modern stuff looks almost as crazy to me as to him, but I still have to give it a chance. I hope to God I outlive this trend. . . . A stab of arthritic pain ripped along her arm and she thought wearily, I've already lived too long. They're going back to the Stone Age, and I can't go along. It's too rough and savage and senseless. . . . Her built-in resilience surged up. You'll feel better after a good dinner . . . pick up some Brie for dessert . . . or fresh strawberries and kirsch . . . twenty of five already . . . if I get a ticket for parking by that fire hydrant, Nicky will have to fix it . . . no, McDougal would raise hell about cops playing favorites . . . I'll send the ticket to Grace and tell her to pay because it was all her fault. . . .

Grace was looking raptly at the screen.

"Grace spotted this one in Portugal—in a Lisbon gallery—and it's a beauty. We thought for the edge of a pool."

It was a rather charming, rough-textured, green stone fish that seemed to be standing on its gills, open-mouthed. At least Lucy found it charming. She began to feel more hopeful about the garden-to-be.

The slide after the fish did nothing to encourage this hope: a dozen fiercely pointed scimitar shapes all tangled up like Laocoön. Davin, sensing the almost concerted reaction of his audience, said tersely, "Ten feet high, steel, done with an oxyacetylene torch. Called 'Touch Therapy.'"

"'Touché Therapy' is more like it," Alec said, in an all-too-audible aside.

Lucy was torn between wanting to laugh and wince. Alec was really being too naughty. She glanced at Grace and thought, It's odd I never realized before she has Sam's jaw.

Alec shrugged. "Sorry. I'm fud-dud about most modern sculpture, and that isn't my department anyway."

Davin said, "No, fortunately, it isn't."

Martha Teague flexed her sturdy ankles and bounded up again. "Couldn't we have the parking lot and put the sculpture around the edges for decoration?"

Davin snapped, "You can't be serious." That seemed to finish Martha.

Lucy said to the room at large, "Why don't we keep most of Sandini's rose garden and scatter the sculpture around in it?"

"Like thorns?" Davin smiled at her, and his tone softened. "Mrs. Ramsdale, you're letting sentimentality muck up your judgment. Come now, *you* know better."

Flora said in a pit-a-pat voice, "We could plant trees as a setting for the—er—the art."

"We wouldn't be able to see the art for the trees. We'd lose the clear, stark effect we're after."

George Farmington had donned the mantle of genial mediator. "But are we sure that's the effect we're after? After all, Wingate is Colonial in architecture, and so is this Center. And we might give a thought to sculpture preserving that tradition."

"You mean like an old Revolutionary cannon?" Davin's eyebrows were expressive. "And why not a wooden Indian too? Then we could shoot the Indian out of the cannon four times a day. That would really have clout. It would bring the art lovers running."

George sat down heavily. Fred Thorndike shoved his pipe into his pocket and stood up, shoulders back, feet together, little moustache stiff with anger. "I understand you're a Californian, Lowry, and of course there's no tradition out there. Push is the order of the day, even in your cemeteries. But here we have a heritage we're justly proud of, and I think George is right. We

35

could collect a group of pieces that would be more in keeping."

"Like Edsel cars for your parking lot? A pity Grace and I didn't think of that when we were spending weeks planning this project. And we've already bought most of the pieces."

"George is chairman of the board of trustees," Myra said angrily. "He ought to have some say in the decision."

"But I'm president and majority stockholder," Grace said. "As George well knows." George tried to smile and nod, but his face crumpled with the effort.

Myra wouldn't be silenced. "Fred was contributing his services."

"Davin's contributing his."

"Yes, I'm *sure* he is." The innuendo came on loud and clear. Grace flushed, then went white.

"But to let a casual outsider come in and dictate to us—" Myra went on.

"As soon as Davin and I are married, I intend to turn over all my stock to him."

All Grace's listeners looked startled, but Lucy had the impression that Davin was more than startled: he was scared, like a cornered mouse.

But then he smiled brilliantly, and Lucy thought, what a statue *he'd* make. I'd like to sketch him. She began to commit him to memory.

Sergeant Terrizi parked the police sedan in Lucy's driveway just after four o'clock, and McDougal abandoned the butterfly bushes he'd been attacking with pruning shears, savagely, to take his visitor around to the studio behind the house.

The big, tranquil room, its uncluttered space soaring two stories high, did nothing to tone down the sergeant's agitated manner. "Angie's uncle is so mad he's spitting knives."

It took the inspector a moment to identify Angie's uncle as the genial owner of Sandini's nursery, where he'd bought red and white impatiens plants the day before, for a shady spot by the terrace. He had hoped the sergeant had come to ask his advice on some gripping police matter that would take his mind off his own problems and set it to ticking clearly. He wasn't in the mood to hear about anybody's uncle. On the grounds of hospitality— "I'll get us a beer"—he retreated to the small kitchen to gain time and, he hoped, the patience needed to listen.

Lucy's stormy departure after the "selfish introvert pig" taunt had shaken his painfully rebuilt sense of balance and left him feeling unwanted. Her accusation had hit all the harder because it carried reverberations of Eileen's "You never want to go anywhere unless somebody's been murdered." Not that there was any real comparison; Eileen had been his wife, and she'd been entitled to have her husband escort her around. If not legally entitled, at least by unwritten law. Lucy was his landlady, and the rented studio, the garden, were the haven he'd settled into after the grim first months of self-imposed exile in a motel room. So he owed Lucy something, and for the past hour he'd been adding up the returns he'd already made. Who was it who'd hired a professional outfit to spray the trees? McDougal, that's who. And who was it who kept her pachysandra and marigolds from being eaten head first by rabbits? He, James McDougal. And who'd cricked his back shoveling snow and chopping wood and putting hot cloths on the water pipes under the sink when they froze? It had seemed quite an impressive list, especially after he'd gone over each item, embroidering, building his defenses. But he was damned if he'd be trotted off on a leash to some chichi opening of an art show. If all she wanted was a gigolo, she could get herself a swish tenant. In his depressed state, it seemed all too likely Lucy might do just that. She'd evict a retired inspector of police who had worked himself to the bone for her, and turn the studio over to somebody who'd bounce on tiptoe and drool silly adjectives—*fabulous, kicky*—and escort her to art shows and concerts and gibbering foreign movies.

As McDougal looked around the little kitchen he'd kept tidy as a ship's galley, he had that wistful this-is-the-last-time feeling of a vacationer who must leave the rented idyll of a summer cottage.

Terrizi hadn't sat down; he took a gulp of beer and spilled out words like a suitcase bursting open: "Sandini came charging into headquarters yelling I got to get a summons to stop them tearing out his roses. It's a crime, all right—those are the greatest roses you'll see in a month of Mondays—but I can't go slapping a summons on a dame for changing her garden. She owns the place."

Usually Terrizi was a model giver of facts, colorful but crisp, but this seemed to be a highly charged issue. "Sandini was supposed to give Angie away at the church in September, but he says if I don't arrest the board of trustees and God knows who all he won't give her away."

"So get another uncle to do the honors." It was McDougal's

belief that in Italian households there was always a surplus of uncles.

A cloud of despair settled over the sergeant's young face. His terra-cotta coloring, even his crackling black hair and eyes, seemed to dim with suffering. "You don't know Angie's mother. She thinks her brother Mario and the Pope and Frank Sinatra—they can do no wrong. I mean, she thinks with her head but her head's like a pot of spaghetti. She didn't want Angie to marry a cop in the first place."

Neither did Eileen's family want her to marry a cop, McDougal thought bitterly. Maybe they were right. I was twelve years older and I had no business tangling with a Junior Leaguer who thought all jobs were nine to five with time off for good behavior.

He wrenched his thoughts away, and back to his guest.

"Angie thinks there's nobody like you. You believed her last summer when nobody else did. Not even me, the prize *idiota*."

The inspector conjured up a mental picture of Angie with real pleasure (impersonal pleasure, of course), and even before the sergeant finished, "So if you'd talk to her—" he was saying, "I'd be glad to," then heard, too late, the last word of the sentence "—mother." Talking to Angie's mother was a different kettle of fish.

He said in what he hoped was a calmly judicial tone, "I'd rather talk to Angie."

"Who wouldn't?"

"But Angie's the one to decide whether to marry you."

"Oh, she'll marry me all right. But that's not the point. She's a real family girl—those Vellas and Sandinis are closer than an octopus to itself. Mario's lived with them since his wife died. And if he and her mama are off me, it's gonna be rough." Even in his agitation, he was careful to put down his beer glass in a large ashtray so it wouldn't mark the table. "I may have to resign from the force and take Angie to live in another town. Maybe another country."

"You can't do that." He'd been unexpectedly jabbed in a vulnerable spot. Except for Lucy, Nicky Terrizi was the only person he felt really close to in Wingate. The sergeant had drawn him into a murder case, and Terrizi's hero worship and eagerness to learn had been healing balm. The inspector couldn't say any of that. "Chief Salter told me the other day you're one of the best cops he ever worked with. You're needed here on the force."

His visitor looked gratified, briefly; then gloom descended again. "The chief's sure no help right now. He said if it's a choice between Mario and Miss Dilworth, he doesn't have to flip a dollar bill to find out who wins. She owns the property. And it's no use talking to her, because she's like her old man—flowers don't mean a thing. When I was working with Mario on their yard"—*yard* was a rather simplified description of the rolling acres next door —"she'd be out there practicing with her rifle, and once she shot the heads off a whole row of marigolds."

"Good God." McDougal was genuinely shocked. "She's worse than rabbits."

"And another time, she was jumping her horse over the iris bed when I'm in there weeding. I'll say for her—she cleared me by a foot. But it didn't exactly make me love her."

McDougal said, wonderingly, "And that's what Lucy wanted me to marry."

Sergeant Terrizi's face expressed a schizoid split in loyalties— astonishment, horror for his friend, then a look of Machiavellian cunning. "It's that guy of hers who's the snake in the ointment. Somebody like you—you'd never put it into her head to tear up Mario's rose garden."

"I am not going to marry Miss Dilworth just to make your in- laws stop fighting."

"No, I can see your point. I mean, just because she's got a lotta dough—and she can be bighearted when she wants to. She used to let me ride her bicycle when I was a kid. And she's not bad- looking, if you're tall enough to take her."

"You're as bad as Lucy."

The sergeant grinned with the fondly rueful air Lucy's name often evoked. "That Mrs. Ramsdale. When she really puts her mind to something—pow. Did you remember to tell her about the engagement party?"

"I told her. But it's the same night as the opening of some art show at the Center, so her idea was that I take her to that and then we'd go on to the party." He lifted his beer glass in an unconscious act of defiance. "I told her the art show was out. She can go alone."

"So what did she say?" the sergeant asked with interest.

"She called me a selfish introvert pig."

Terrizi chuckled, then decided that might be disrespectful and changed it to an unconvincing cough.

"And she practically said she'd kick me out and find a new tenant." He stared gloomily at the wall of books flanking the big fieldstone fireplace.

The sergeant, watching him, remembered when the inspector had got his own books out of storage in Hartford, and had spent a week contentedly arranging them by subject matter. Terrizi still had the borrowed Volume XI of *Famous British Trials*. I'll have more time to read, he thought, when Angie goes back on the four-to-midnight shift at the answering service. Maybe he'd let me take the Gonzalez that's got all the poisons, the one we looked up the digitalis in. . . . He ought to get back to work. If our boys had another big case breaking . . . but these crazy kids sniffing hair spray in a paper bag for a cheap high—so some of them drop dead, poor little devils, but it's not like a real big . . . he found he was thinking wishfully of some juicy homicide he could offer the inspector on a platter, like the head of St. John the Baptist. He crossed himself hurriedly, surreptitiously, but his host was too sunk in misery to notice.

Terrizi said gently, "Whenever Mrs. Ramsdale gets mad she means what she says, but she never means it for more than ten minutes. Like when I was working for her, if she bawled me out, pretty soon she'd be bringing out fresh-baked brownies."

"She can't buy me off with brownies. That doesn't excuse her tantrums."

"It doesn't excuse them, but to tell you the truth, she's not a lady you can make excuses for. She just *is*. She's proud as they come, and she'd feel hurt you didn't want to take her to this fancy opening." The sergeant had thought of another reason, totally unaltruistic, for promoting peace.

41

"She knows how I feel about those gabbeta-gabbeta affairs."

"Yeah, but she's probably scared to go by herself."

"She wouldn't be scared of a herd of charging rhinoceri, and that's almost as bad as an art opening."

"The thing is, it's not safe for a woman to go out alone now, at night. Say, you know what I bought Angie today in Danbury? Wait'll I show you. It's in the car."

He raced out and came back with a large black flashlight. "For nights when she gets off at midnight and I can't pick her up. Watch." He pressed, and a light like a beacon came on, blindingly. McDougal was about to make some polite comment when the high-pitched wail of a police siren sounded, and on long-time reflex, he jumped. The sergeant said proudly, "Pretty good, isn't it? The mugger hears that and scrams."

Like most men, the inspector couldn't resist gadgets. He reached for the flashlight and pushed buttons like a five-year-old. "Smart idea. It's a lot more effective than a whistle in a handbag."

"You oughta get Mrs. Ramsdale one. Frail little lady like her, having to run around by herself at night . . . tell you what—you take this one for her and I'll pick up another for Angie."

As four dollars and sixty-nine cents changed hands, the inspector said, "She'll push buttons and have me leaping up at all hours when the siren blasts off." But the truth was he could hardly wait to show Lucy her present.

"You got any idea when she'll be back?"

"She may stop for a drink with those two men down the road."

"Foster and Melton? Say, Bert Melton called the chief today about an old weather vane somebody'd brought into Way Back Antiques to sell. Melton said it looked like the old rooster on top of Town Hall. He'd sold them that one in the first place. And you know what, it *was* the rooster on top of Town Hall. They'd never even missed it. Seems this is a new hot racket: somebody rents a helicopter and goes around lifting weather vanes off roofs. You'd be surprised at how much an antique weather vane brings."

"I wouldn't be surprised at anything in the antique business. Some of those dealers are pirates."

"Not Bert Melton. He's as honest as the night is long. Ask Mrs.

Ramsdale. She's sent a lot of summer people to that store since he came. You know how she is—anything for a friend."

The inspector had a sudden flashback of Lucy in a pale pink smock, sitting on the floor of the studio, packing carton after carton of her dead husband's books and labeling them with a drawing pencil in her scrawling uphill writing. It couldn't have been easy for her, but she'd insisted McDougal must have room for his own books. "I doubt if you'd want your furniture moved down here because it's so haunted. You'd always see double when you looked at it—you'd see your wife sitting and lying with you, all over the place." Even her bluntness had been therapeutic. And she'd been right about the books. Maybe he'd been too adamant. After all, she hadn't had an easy time of it herself. And if he'd hurt her pride. . . .

The sergeant had the Italian gift of empathy. In a coaxing voice, he said, "It might not be so bad, going to that art show. You could just go around with your eyes closed or something."

McDougal snorted, but since he was being given advice that fitted his revised line of thinking, he was inclined to accept it. "I suppose it wouldn't hurt me this once."

"Great." The sergeant's beaming pleasure touched McDougal, until he caught the whiff of ulterior motive. "I'd sure appreciate it if you talked to her tonight about saving Mario's rose garden. That would help a lot more than talking to Angie's mother, because all you could tell Angie's mother is that my hands are tied, legally." The sergeant's hands, as he talked, were anything but tied; he was a second-generation Italian American, but the outflung gestures predated the Appian Way.

"I gotta get back to the gristmill. Thanks for letting me blow my cool. I feel a helluva lot better now. If anybody can fix things up for Mario, it's Mrs. Ramsdale. Would it be O.K. if I borrowed your *Toxicology* for a little light reading? I can curl up with it nights while Angie's on the four-to-midnight shift. I want to brush up on my poisons."

He wasn't tall enough to reach the shelf it was on. (He had passed the police entrance requirement on minimum height by, almost literally, a hair.) McDougal took down the heavy volume

43

and handed it over. "Just don't pick up any pointers on bumping off Angie's mother."

"Not me. She cooks too good." He patted his sturdy middle. "You'd better save up for our party. Don't eat for twenty-four hours before. Manicotti—*spiedini alla griglia*—that's veal roll with prosciutto—roasted artichokes—*muzatta*—*pesche* stuffed with almonds. . . ."

After Terrizi had gone, the inspector felt gnawingly hungry. He debated whether to fix himself something, but Lucy always called if she wasn't coming home for dinner, and when she was there she usually asked him to eat with her. He much preferred her cooking to his own.

When he went in to shower, he left the bathroom door open so that he could hear if the phone rang. He was lathering himself enthusiastically with Yardley bath soap when the phone jangled. The soap slid out of his hand and waylaid him on the wet tiles so that he skidded violently. Cursing and dripping, he groped his way to the phone.

"Inspector? Terrizi there?"

It was Chief Salter of the Wingate police. Not Lucy. In his relief, McDougal became almost chatty, estimating the exact minute of the sergeant's departure and his probable arrival time at headquarters. He felt rather envious as he said, "Any special trouble?"

"Mario Sandini got stoned and he's leaping in and out of traffic on Main Street, waving a bush. I figured Terrizi could persuade him to go along quietly. Otherwise we'll have to book him for sure. He already assaulted a cop with a rosebush. You think that's funny, you oughta see the scratches . . . oh, here's the sergeant now. Thanks."

McDougal finished his shower in high good humor and put on a sport shirt Lucy had given him for his birthday after she'd looked up the date on his driver's license. He had thought the shirt was on the gaudy side, beige with enormous black dots, but tonight it looked more acceptable. Five fifty. If Lucy hadn't called by now, she'd be home any minute. Six ten . . . six nineteen . . . by six thirty-five, McDougal was so unnerved he got out the phone book to look up Alec Foster's number. Busy. Bizzy, bizzy, bizzy. Probably Foster or Melton inviting nine other people to come have dinner there with Lucy.

He poured himself a stiff slug of Scotch and had taken one tasteless sip when he heard the imperious honk of the Saab. Lucy was home. *Honk, honk, honk.* That meant she needed a hand.

His long legs covered the ground to the front driveway in roughly twenty-nine seconds. From there he sauntered to her car. It had begun to drizzle, and her white hair was curling in the dampness.

"Mac, will you help me with this stuff?" She loaded him like a Christmas tree with packages. "Don't let the chicken drip on that shirt. I'm going to make dumplings—I'd planned anchovy-and-onion tarts, but we'll have them tomorrow instead."

Bribing with fresh-baked brownies, McDougal said silently. But he couldn't feel really mad.

"Will you make me a drink? And bring yours to the kitchen while I get things started. It's been the most horrible afternoon. The meeting went on forever."

While she kneaded dough for the dumplings, quickly and deftly, on the board that pulled out of the counter, she gave him highlights of the meeting. "So now Alec's broody and the Farmingtons are livid. Fred Thorndike looked as if he'd slap Davin's cheek with a gauntlet and stalk twenty paces at dawn. And the worst thing is, I couldn't do a damn thing about Mario's rose garden. I tried to talk to Grace again after the meeting. But the United Parcel truck unloaded some crates—those metal atrocities they call sculpture—and Davin raced down to open them, and Grace was so anxious to join him she couldn't even be civil. I wanted to find Mario to explain, but he'd vanished. I could have wept."

This was no moment to tell her about Angie's uncle assaulting a cop with a rosebush. Lucy had already done her best to save the garden; nobody could do anything more. The inspector's conscience flipped clear of its assigned task; the sergeant would understand. Angie's mother could sublimate her fury by cooking a mountain of pasta for the party.

Lucy's chicken was simmering fragrantly in an earthenware pot. The rain-freshened breeze through the back screen door was pleasantly cool. And his drink no longer tasted medicinal; it was convivial.

"Grace really would do anything to please that man. I never saw anybody so besotted. When you've been a virgin that long, it hits you much harder. Like a grown man getting the mumps. Well, not like that, but backwards. She even announced right at the meeting they were going to be married. But I have a feeling he doesn't really want to."

"Neither do I want to," the inspector said firmly.

"But I think maybe for different reasons." Lucy sounded preoccupied. Then she shook her head, as if airing it of murky thoughts, and drained her glass. "Will you make me another? I shouldn't, but I need it. I feel sunk."

She, who usually sat so straight, was hunched over wearily. When McDougal said gruffly he'd got her a little present, she slid to the edge of her chair and sparkled. "Lovely. You couldn't have picked a better day. Where is it?"

But when he brought out the flashlight, her face crumpled with disappointment. "I already have two."

"Not like this one. Press the red button."

The peaceful June dusk was ripped by the screech of sirens, and Lucy was enchanted. Her dark blue eyes glinted mischievously. "I know why you gave it to me. But with this, who needs a police escort in the evenings?" McDougal cleared his throat, ready to lay his head on the block—on a temporary basis—when she said, "Anyway, the art show's been canceled. They're going to be tearing up the whole back of the place starting tomorrow. So we can go straight to Angie's party. I'm so glad she isn't a nun."

The inspector thought of saying, You're not as glad as Nicky. It was rather a pity, though, that Angie wasn't an orphan.

"She was meant to get married and have babies and live noisily ever after. But if somebody isn't—" She snatched up the flashlight and pressed the red button again. Above the din she yelled, "It sounds the way I feel." When she shut it off, she looked happier, as if she'd been to a wailing wall and had a good response.

She was patting bits of dough into balls when the phone rang. "Get it, Mac, will you? My hands are sticky."

McDougal answered on the extension in the hall just outside the kitchen and came back wearing a dour Scots expression. "For you."

"If it's Flora Pollit, I'm out."

"It's no Flora. It's a throbbing male voice."

Lucy leaped, light as a girl, snatching a paper towel on the way. The inspector was left staring at a lump of dough, but began to feel better when he heard her say, "Not tonight—I'm exhausted after all that wrangling, and we haven't started dinner yet. . . . All right, tomorrow, but I do my stint at the Thrift Shop until five. . . . Yes, five thirty."

She hung up with a slam of impatience. "Davin Lowry wanted to come spill his troubles to his 'eccentric aunt next door.' I resent being anybody's 'eccentric aunt,' especially—" She stopped, then said, "Oh!" and burst out laughing. "But I offered to be his aunt before the meeting. I wonder. . . ." She rolled another blob of dough and regarded the little thing dreamily. "Well, I'll know tomorrow."

But by the next day, Davin Lowry wasn't saying a word.

5

The inspector didn't believe in sleeping pills. He had disapproved of his wife's taking even one Nembutal at night, and he'd lectured her more than once on the danger of taking pills after she'd had several drinks. During the year and a half since the breakup of their marriage, when the nights too often stretched out in the endless black bog of memories, he had denied himself sternly, almost masochistically, the pill panacea. Gardening, and chores around Lucy's place, had made it easier to get to sleep, but insomnia still lurked in the shadows, waiting to yank him tensely awake around 2 A.M.

He had learned not to lie in darkness, sliding deeper and deeper into the bog. Instead, he put on the bedside light and read for an hour or two. For some reason—which might be worthy of scientific research—the books he often found most soothing were cookbooks. Not the Casseroles for Busy Bustlers sort, but the more exotic breed. He didn't read them for practical purposes; his own cooking was of the steaks, chops, and hamburgers variety, with an occasional soup. But he read them as an armchair traveler leafs through brochures with vivid illustrations and even more highly colored descriptions of remote places that are better at a safe distance.

He had been careful not to mention this nocturnal vice to Lucy, although he should have known that trying to keep a secret from Lucy was like standing in front of an X-ray machine in a gauzy whiffle. The time he'd unearthed an old, broken-spine copy of *Mrs. Beeton's Cookbook* in a stack of donations in the Second Run Thrift Shop, where Lucy worked as a volunteer, she had seen him sneak a look at the price pencil-marked in the front and leave twice that amount, surreptitiously, on a counter, so that he could feel right about smuggling the book out in a plain wrapper—that is, in his raincoat pocket. So far, Lucy hadn't said a word.

She knew he read late at night; she had seen his light go on and stay on. Lucy herself always read murder mysteries at bedtime. (She had once met a favorite mystery writer at a cocktail party and told him that, and he had said he was sick and tired of hearing it—made him feel like a sedative.) She had urged the inspector to help himself to her collection of whodunits, but he would as soon have eaten Crunchy Wunchies in bed. He regarded any fictional murder as pap.

When Lucy tried to push a new lending-library thriller at him an hour or so after the chicken and dumplings, McDougal yawned and said he was going right to sleep.

And he did, after a brief turn around the garden. The rain had stopped. Two new bronze iris had opened since midafternoon, and a white edged with purple, luminously lovely in the light of an almost full moon. He was vaguely aware of a car turning out of the driveway next door, and soon afterwards, of a woman's silhouette in an upstairs window. Grace Whosis, who was bulldozing a rose garden to please her fiancé. Better him than me, the inspector thought contentedly, and went to bed.

It was a double bed in the studio's little bedroom, and it took up too much space, but McDougal preferred it for at least two reasons. He and Eileen had always slept in twin beds, and the sight of a flatly empty bed next his own would have peopled the place with haunts. Once when he and his wife had been invited for a weekend with friends who had a summer cottage at the shore, he had heard her telling their hostess, in her exuberantly exaggerated way, that she and Mac couldn't sleep double "because the few times we've had to, either we each lie rigidly

49

on an edge, or we roll in and end up making love most of the night, which can be awfully tiring."

The advantage now of the double bed was that by lying at a slant, McDougal could uncoil to his full six feet three and not have to curl like a fetus to avoid hitting the footboard.

He slept in this loose-angled sprawl for at least three hours, before he woke with that ominous, tight-wound feeling of, I'm in for it. He turned on his reading light and looked at his watch: one twenty-five. Conrad's *Lord Jim* lay on his bedside table, but this was more for show. He was keeping Mrs. Beeton in the drawer. He upended his pillows, arranged them one behind the other, and prepared to uncurl with a recipe.

For an author who had so many genteel tips on footmen, Mrs. Beeton seemed rather bloodthirsty: "The best and most humane mode of killing a hog is to strike it down with the pointed end of a pole-axe on the forehead. . . . Choose a small leg of pork, cut and slit, and fill with sage and onion stuffing. . . ." On roast moorfowl, she commanded, "Cut off the heads and toes. . . . Cover the breast with vine leaves and bacon. . . ."

The screech of the siren was so incongruous with roast moorfowl that it seemed to blast off practically in his ear. It took him a second to realize it *was* practically in his ear, or at least right on the premises. Lucy! He leaped up, pulled on his pants, and tucked in his pajama top as he ran.

Lucy was leaning out an upstairs window waving her flashlight howler like a club. She turned off the siren to make herself heard. "Mac, there's somebody trying to steal my car."

McDougal's first thought was that no one, not even a hopped-up moron, would bother stealing Lucy's Saab. He had bawled her out repeatedly for leaving her keys in the car in an unlocked garage, but it had been more a matter of principle than of active alarm. She must be having wishful delusions so she could try out her new toy. As he loped down the driveway and approached the garage head on, Lucy's Saab hurtled out like a jack rabbit and nearly ran him down before his professional instincts were aroused. Also his wrath. He shouted, "Stop or I'll shoot." He had nothing to shoot with—not on him—but it sounded authoritative.

The Saab's brakes jerked screechily to a halt, and its headlights blinked on. A woman's voice said, "Oh, I'm so sorry if I woke you, Lucy. I wanted to borrow your car. Did you call the police? The siren. . . ."

"It's my own siren." There was the smugness of pride in Lucy's voice, before concern took over. "Grace dear, what's wrong?"

Grace emerged in sections from the tiny car, after untangling her legs from the gearshift. She was wearing dark slacks and a pullover, and her face was so white it looked almost phosphorescent in the moonlight. "Davin took my car hours ago, to go in to the Arts Center. He'd forgotten the slides, and he said he'd just pick them up and take a few measurements in the garden and be right back. When he didn't come, I got so panicky. I thought you wouldn't mind if I took your car. I was going to leave it in front afterward and not wake you. I'm terribly sorry."

Grace's voice had always been on the high side, but now it was shrill, quivering with near hysteria.

"Dear, of course I don't mind. But you're in no condition to drive in alone at this hour. Mac—Mac, where are you?"

McDougal, who had stepped back into the shadow of the garage to make sure his fly was zippered and to finish tucking in his pajama top, came forward in bare feet but otherwise decently covered.

Lucy, hanging out the bedroom window clutching her thin robe around her shoulders, made the introductions.

"Mac, you'll drive her in, won't you?"

Ordinarily, the inspector would have resisted Lucy's ordering him around, but this was like asking a fireman if he wanted to go to a fire. McDougal was definitely interested. "I'd be glad to."

"Oh, he mustn't. Really. I couldn't think of it. And I didn't want to call the police because Davin would be cross if I made a big thing. . . ."

"Mac's not police. He's retired."

The words cut through McDougal's mind and left jagged edges. It was one thing to be retired; it was another to be called that.

51

"It seems like an awful imposition, but if you're sure you wouldn't mind." Her voice was softer now, and she looked much younger than McDougal had pictured her, not at all like a woman who would shoot the heads off marigolds. Her dark hair was pulled back and tied with a ribbon, ponytail fashion. Her eyes seemed enormous in her pale face. And she was tall and slim as an adolescent boy, in the slacks and sweater. "I—I can use help. If Davin isn't at the Center, we could cruise around. He might have stopped in a bar."

"We'll go in my car. Take me five minutes."

He kept his own car beside the studio in summer and, in fact, till as late in the season as he dared. Lucy's garage theoretically held two cars, but it was so crammed with gardening tools, sacks of fertilizer, a broken-legged easel, outdoor cushions, flats for seedlings, and inefficient bug sprays that only the threat of a blizzard made him seek cover. When he drove the Buick around to the front, four and a half minutes later, Lucy was standing in the driveway in a long, pale blue robe, cradling a bottle of brandy. "Mac, have a slug." She thrust the bottle through his car window with a stack of paper cups. "I made Grace drink some. And take the bottle along—like a Saint Bernard."

McDougal thought she was being determinedly cheerful. He had never seen her in a robe and slippers before, and she looked smaller and more fragile. Or perhaps it was because she was standing beside Grace.

"Davin probably just lost track of time. Hal used to do that. I'd have to go haul him out of the studio at all hours of the night when he was working. Why don't you bring Davin back here for coffee and scrambled eggs, and I'll tell him what I think of him for worrying you silly."

Grace smiled wanly and got into the seat beside McDougal. "He'll listen more to you. He raved about you tonight."

"Well, he raved about you to me."

"Did he?" She made an odd, choked sound. "You aren't just saying that?"

McDougal gunned the motor as a noisy hint to cut off the chitchat. He resented their using up moments he'd saved by not

52

putting on a shirt; even with a jacket over his pajama top, he felt *déshabillé*, and his shoes, without socks, clammed to his feet.

"Are you warm enough, dear? Would you like a coat?"

His hackles bristled. Entirely too possessive. Lucy had never called him "dear" before. He realized belatedly she was talking to his passenger.

Grace said she was warm enough. But on the way into town, she began to shiver uncontrollably. "He w-will be all right, w-won't he?"

"I certainly hope so." Neither of them said much else. McDougal was relieved that Grace wasn't the sort who babbled. Hysteria usually took women that way. In his years as a cop, he had preferred subduing armed thugs to hysterical females. Quite apart from that, he disliked talking, or being talked at, when he was driving. His wife had complained he might as well be wearing blinders and earplugs when they went any place in a car. She had kept calling his attention to irrelevant scenery and what she called amusing signs. And perversely, now that she was gone, he was constantly seeing the things she would have spotted and exclaimed over.

Soon after he turned off the side road onto the interstate highway, his headlights picked up a large portable sign on the right: CAUTION: MEN IN TREES. His wife would have ignored the sensible explanation (sign left behind by a telephone repair crew) and been charmed by the threat of wild men pouncing from trees. Grace distracted him from this wistful wooliness by leaning forward abruptly to peer at a car going in the opposite direction. "It was a green Mercedes—I thought for a minute—but mine is a two-eighty. I want to make sure we don't miss him on the road if he's started home."

McDougal reflected that Fairfield County, Connecticut, probably had more Mercedeses per square foot than any place else in the country. Maybe in the world. He had never had the faintest hankering after a Mercedes or its ilk. Some ex-Presbyterian strain in his Scottish blood chilled to the fast flash of eaten-up money and mileage. The solid anonymity of his Buick suited him fine, and the special engine. As if redeclaring allegiance, he let the speedometer slide up to seventy, while the highway unrolled in easy curves through the wet green coolness of trees. The moon rode high, golden, serene, as if it had never been jumped on except by ancient gods. He hadn't been out that late in over a year, and he began to feel boyishly exhilarated. The fact that he wasn't alone, that his passenger was a woman with a striking profile and no middle-age bulge, made it distinctly more adventurous.

Even Wingate's Main Street, by daytime in summer a hooting, smelly, darting line of cars, looked fascinatingly different. Most of the store windows had only dim night lights: Go home, all is forgiven; neither buying nor selling attend ye till the morrow. Coleman's Market, where he and Lucy shopped, was so mysteriously, flittily lit, it looked like a waterfront dive.

He turned off Main onto Bayard Street and drove toward the Arts Center in the next block. Grace let out a little moan. "No car. He can't be here. The place is dark."

"Dark" wasn't quite the word McDougal would have used. The illuminated sign over the entrance, DILWORTH ARTS AND CRAFTS CENTER, was blatantly bright among the sleeping houses around it, and the brass eagle looked as if it were about to take off in the neon's white glare. But as he parked his car in front, he saw that all the windows were dark.

"Is there a night watchman?"

"No. And the janitor goes home at five. I tipped him today so he'd stay to help Davin open the crates."

"Did you bring a key?" He was exasperated he hadn't thought of that at the start.

"I don't have one. Alec and the janitor—oh, Fred Thorndike must still have one. But I can't ask Fred to come over and open it for us. I can't. Really, I can't." Her voice was getting the shakes again, and she kept brushing her hand across her cheek.

McDougal used his quietest tone. "That isn't necessary. I can always get a skeleton key at headquarters. But you haven't told me how Lowry could get into the building."

"Oh, it was open till after ten, for a concert. And he said all he had to do was pick up the slides and . . . but I didn't want him to go. I shouldn't have let him. I wanted to come along, but I was trying not to be possessive. His mother was awful that way. He said she was like a combination of eiderdown and bloodsucker."

Had Davin Lowry been so leery of marriage he'd run home to crawl under that eiderdown bloodsucker? McDougal was debating how to word this tactfully—Do you think your fiancé ran off in your car and is heading for Mama? wasn't quite it—when Grace said in a matter-of-fact tone, "She's dead."

So that took care of Mama. McDougal reached across and took a flashlight out of the glove compartment. "I won't be long."

"But if the car isn't here . . . maybe we should drive by the Inn first. He might have stopped for a drink."

"We can go there next."

As he got out of the car, she said, "I can't sit here doing nothing—I've had hours of just sitting. Let me come with you."

"All right." She went ahead of him up the wet cobblestone path, walking in long strides, as long as his own, then stood aside to let him try the front door. Locked. But McDougal still went through the motions of rattling the knob and banging. "Halloo. Anybody there?"

"Davin wouldn't have stayed. He'd have left before the place was locked up for the night."

McDougal said, "I'll take a look around the garden—and isn't there a vacant lot behind? Will you show me?"

Grace led the way to the side path which made a half circle around the left of the building and ended at the stone steps leading down to the garden. The scent of roses, fresh after rain, drifted up to them.

Lucy had said earlier that week, "Mac, you absolutely must go and see those roses before they get blowsy," but he wasn't a rose man by nature. And he was still scratchy from clearing dead brambles out of Lucy's ramblers along the stone wall; the thorns had jabbed even through work gloves.

Now, looking down from the top of the steep stairs to the garden silvered in moonlight, it wasn't the beauty that held him; it was the inky section at the bottom of the steps, in the shadow of the rose arbor. And he had a sudden strong instinct not to use his flashlight yet. "I'll go down and check things out."

"Hang onto the—" Grace began, just as he skidded on the top step. Grace grabbed his arm in a reassuringly hard grip and steadied him. Having already skidded in the shower that afternoon, he was doubly annoyed. He said "Thanks," or grunted it, without gratitude.

And he hung onto the railing like a cautious old woman the rest of the way down.

"Better put on your flashlight so you won't stumble. We left everything scattered around in a mess when the rain started."

Even before he switched on his light, McDougal could see it was a mess, all right. The messiest feature was Davin Lowry, impaled through the neck on the prongs of "Touch Therapy."

6

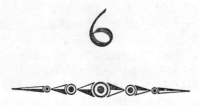

Sergeant Terrizi was having a hideous dream: he was standing in front of the altar resplendent in rented attire and a white carnation, waiting for his pretty bride to come down the aisle on the arm of her Uncle Mario. But what came down the aisle was a large bush waddling along on Angie's feet in satin slippers. Like a variation of Birnam wood to Dunsinane, but much nastier for a bridegroom.

In his distress, the sergeant moaned and plucked at a sheet. The bush advanced nearer and grabbed him in a thorny hug.

"Nicky! Nicky! *Ascolti.*"

It was his mother, Gorgon-headed with curlers, shaking him awake. A soft, drifting wave of thankfulness washed over him: he had not married a bush. His mother was talking up a storm in Italian, but his ears still floated in that muzzy state between sleep and lucid thinking. He was used to her waking him at odd hours. She often heard noises in the night (her imagination was very noisy), and as she had once said, "Your papa needs his sleep. You're the cop. You go look."

Tonight's awakening wasn't as rude as most, in that it had snatched him from a fate worse than death: marrying an aggressive green thing instead of Angie. So he grumbled only mildly as he sat up in bed.

"You get on your uniform and you jump down those stairs *presto.*"

"My uniform," he said dazedly. This was going rather far even for Mama. Until now, she had never insisted on his donning official regalia instead of his usual night attire—pajama bottoms—to trot downstairs and confront a mythical prowler.

"With the Inspector McDougal waiting, you go naked-chested as a jay bird?"

Long before "bird," Sergeant Terrizi had vaulted out of bed, made a dive for the closet, and was frantically yanking out the hangers that held his prized uniform. "Why the hell didn't you tell me he was waiting?" He could see the inspector pacing the small confines of the Terrizi's front parlor. He grabbed shorts from a chair by his bed.

"So now you decide to wear dirty underwear. You got ten pairs of clean ones in a drawer, but you meet the inspector in dirty underwear."

"They're not dirty," he shouted. "I only put them on last night before I went out with Angie."

His mother said cryptically, "Don't tell me—I do the wash."

In his haste and embarrassment, the sergeant thrust both feet into one pants leg, and hopped around like a drunken flamingo. "Mama, will you get out of here? Go tell the inspector I'll be with him in two minutes."

"So you fly like a crow. Ten minutes at least you need to get there. And don't you drive like a maniac or you'll end up wound around a tree like a crazy teen-ager."

Her son, who had graduated from teen-age five years before, got his pants on, one leg to each side, and fumbled with buttons on his tan twill shirt. "Mama, I thought you said the inspector is downstairs waiting."

"Not *him*. He's got better things to do than sit twiddling his little finger while you primp in a mirror."

"I'm only combing my hair," the sergeant said brokenly. "*Who's downstairs?*"

"Why should anybody be downstairs?" his mother inquired in a reasonable tone, then crossed herself hurriedly, as insurance in case a burglar was listening. Her son had inherited her sparkling black eyes and springy curls but, luckily, not her temperament in toto; his father's more placid genes had tempered the volatile mixture. "Will you start at the beginning and just tell me calmly?"

"I am sleeping like a baby with paregorica. The phone rings. Your papa only snores like a walrus. I grab the phone. Detective Waters's voice I hear because he tells me who he is. He begs my pardon *graziosamente* for calling at this hour. Will I ask the sergeant to go to the Artsy Center and meet the inspector. I tell him yes. I come shake you and repeat all he says."

"Didn't he say why the inspector wants me?"

"At three A.M. you think he wants you for trampling grapes into wine? Somebody's dead—you can count on it. Dope addicts shooting innocent people. Nobody's safe. Better the Mafia than this. They only shoot each other."

"Did he actually say somebody was killed?" The sergeant had progressed to his shoes.

"He says 'accident.' So I ask is it Angie's Uncle Mario. Naturally I think of him first because Mario takes care of that garden like a baby. Nights, Sundays. . . ."

"Mario's safe home in bed. I took him home before I picked up Angie. He passed out."

"He passed in again. He's somewhere not in his bed. One brown sock and one gray sock you're wearing. They'll promote you to captain for being so *elegante*. His truck's gone."

By the time the sergeant reached his own getaway car, a 1968 Chevrolet, his nerves were not of the calmest.

His first look at the corpse did nothing to soothe his insides. The sergeant's knowledge of sculpture was largely confined to the Virgin Mary with child, Christ nailed to the cross, and other such normal subjects. The sight of the writhing steel prongs of "Touch Therapy" would have shaken him even without a corpse attached. "Holy Mother," he said in a hoarse whisper, *"That's* a statue? Who's the . . . ?" He looked away from the sickening sight of what had been a man.

"Miss Dilworth's friend Lowry."

"Does she know yet?"

"She saw the body."

The inspector had called to her urgently, "Don't come down," but he hadn't been able to stop her. And he still couldn't forget the whimpering sound, the pitiful, "No. It can't be. He was alive tonight."

McDougal had led her back to his car and made her take a few sips of brandy. Then he'd driven her to the phone booth on the corner and she'd sat frozenly in the front seat while he called police headquarters to report. In turn, the night sergeant had a message for him: "Mrs. Ramsdale said to tell you if anything's wrong, send Miss Dilworth to her house to stay all night." The police doctor, who arrived soon after the first patrol car, had given her a shot of tranquilizer while men roped off the steps and the rose garden. "That ought to knock her out for about eight hours. She's in no condition to be questioned before then."

For once, McDougal was relieved to hear the familiar jargon; he welcomed any postponement on questioning Grace Dilworth. He hadn't known Davin Lowry, but if the gruesome discovery had made even a long-time police inspector queasy, it heightened his awareness of how much more horrible the shock must have been for her. The fact that she hadn't screamed or carried on deepened his sympathy and made him feel strongly protective.

"We'll send her right over to Lucy Ramsdale's. Any instructions?"

"Tell Lucy—oh, go teach your grandmother to suck ostrich eggs. Lucy took my first-aid course when I was still green behind the ears, and she taught me a thing or two. She even invented a new pressure point."

McDougal's sudden grin made him look years younger. He went off for a patrolman to deliver Grace Dilworth safely. "Tell Mrs. Ramsdale what happened and she'll know what to do. The injection will take effect in about a half hour and should last till noon."

As Grace got into the patrol car, she said to McDougal in an exhausted voice, "Thank you for bringing me in. It would have been worse if I'd been alone." Her face, frozen in grief, had the classic beauty of Roman marble.

The police doctor stowed the hypodermic needle away in a shabby black leather kit. "That girl's got iron guts. Sam brought her up to take her medicine like a man. Although, come to think of it, that's a damn-fool statement. A lot of men are the world's biggest babies about taking medicine. Now lead me to your corpse."

It was already the inspector's corpse. Chief Salter had made that clear over the short-wave radio in a patrol car: "Inspector, you found the body, so that's all the more reason for you to take charge. You'd be doing us a big favor. I'll get hold of any state troopers cruising in this area. And if you want Terrizi to help you. . . ."

The sergeant had been brought in through the vacant lot, threading his way through the fresh plaster casts of footprints, dotted whitely around the garden like night-blooming fungi. The police had unlocked the Arts Center and turned on all the outdoor lights: the roses were brilliantly spotlighted. So was "Touch Therapy."

"Nasty, isn't it?" McDougal said to Terrizi in a stringently brisk voice. "Hoist on his own petard."

The sergeant had never tangled with "petard." Another word for statue? He made a mental note to look it up in a dictionary, and this had a steadying effect; it made him feel life was more orderly, more easily defined, than it seemed at the moment. "You mean somebody hoisted him up and threw him on that—that thing?"

"He wasn't hoisted—he fell."

"Then it was an accident, wasn't it?" But why the casts of footprints? And if Mario's prints showed up large and bold in the damp earth, it would mean he'd come back after the rain started. Terrizi repeated almost pleadingly, "Wasn't it an accident?"

The inspector had already been over that with Chief Salter, who had hoped almost as hard as Terrizi that it would turn out to be a case of accidental death but had manfully agreed homicide was "a possibility." Privately, McDougal thought "a probability" was more accurate, but he preferred to let the matter dangle just now.

"The steps were slippery after the rain, and Lowry may have lost his balance. But I'm glad you took Mario home earlier."

The sergeant's Adam's apple bobbled convulsively. "He went out again. Mama just told me. His sister was looking for him around ten." The fact that the sergeant and his date had been parked, at that hour, on a back road euphemistically known as Honeysuckle Lane made him feel even guiltier. "His truck's gone."

"That's—awkward."

"Awkward" was entirely too Nordic a word, under the circumstances. The sergeant felt as if his stomach were being whirled by centrifugal forces. When he had put Mario to bed, over six hours before, Mario had roused enough to mutter, "He's a man from Mars and he's wrecking our planet by tearing up *le rose* . . . gotta get him before it's too late. . . . Tell them for his funeral, 'Please omit . . . omit . . . omit'. . . ." And with a beatific smile, he'd slid into drunken sleep. The sergeant wrenched his mind from this ominous recollection to concentrate on what the inspector was saying.

". . . police doctor thinks Lowry fell headfirst and one of the prongs may have severed his carotid artery. We'll know more after the autopsy. Somebody might have given him a push at the top of the steps."

"You said the steps were slippery," the sergeant reminded him doggedly.

"I skidded on the top one and damn near took a fall. Like stepping on grease or—" McDougal's lean jaw dropped, and his mouth stayed open but no sound came out for almost a minute. "See if one of the men has a knife. Any kind of knife. I've got a crazy idea, and I want to be sure I'm wrong."

As the sergeant trotted off on his errand, he was saying passionately, silently, Let him be wrong. Let it be an accident. The guy Lowry deserved to slip, so he slipped. Another part, the well-trained, law-upholding part of Terrizi, was shocked at such heresy. *A police officer must keep an impartial mind at all times.* But if he had to arrest Angie's uncle . . . I shoulda sat in his room all night to make sure he didn't get out again . . . I shoulda shorted the ignition in his truck . . . I shoulda handcuffed him to the bedpost. . . .

One of the detectives had a switchblade he'd confiscated that night, which he dug out of the trunk of his car. "It's got a little blood on it," he said, apologetically.

The sergeant carried this dubious prize back and found McDougal kneeling in the wet grass beside the top step, his flashlight focusing down and his head bowed so low he looked like a religious suppliant. "Can't see anything here, but I'll take a scraping."

Terrizi explained about the blood. "Would you like me to wash it first?"

The inspector was already shaking his head impatiently. "Rub it in the grass. That should be enough."

When Terrizi handed over the purified contraband, the inspector used the side of the blade to scrape the top step so closely it scrunched like a nail on a blackboard. Then he took a small memo pad out of his jacket pocket, wiped off the blade on the top sheet, and tore off the sheet. "We'll see if the lab finds any traces."

Traces of what? Terrizi was afraid to ask. He watched McDougal fold over the sheet of memo pad, sandwich it between two unused sheets, and put it in his wallet. All sound police procedure. But the next bit smacked of old-line Sherlock Holmes. McDougal scraped the step with a fingernail and then put the finger in his mouth and sucked it thoughtfully. "Mmmm. Scrape the step right here and see what you think it tastes like."

The sergeant squatted reluctantly. For one thing, his mother had instilled in him a horror of germs. And for another thing, he didn't want the top step to taste of anything. But he scraped, sucked his fingernail, and shuddered at the memory evoked: he had been five years old when he'd brought home a lusty new word from the kindergarten playground and had proudly tried it on his mother, whereupon she'd hauled him over to the sink and washed out his mouth till he foamed. "Soap," he said now, sadly. "It sort of tastes of soap."

"That's what I thought, but I could have had a preconceived notion. Let's try a few more."

Only the first and second steps were slippery with soap.

"It doesn't make sense. How could anybody be sure Lowry would be the one to start down the steps? There was a concert here tonight, and anybody might have come out to see the roses and taken a fall. Who'd be crazy enough to take a chance of killing any passer-by?" The sergeant grabbed at this flimsy straw and bent it: "Mario wouldn't ever have done that."

"Not if he was sober, maybe. But he wasn't sober. And if the soap came from here. . . ."

The sergeant had a horrifying mental picture of a cake of soap sitting not ten feet away, beside an outdoor faucet, where he'd often seen Mario wash his hands and dry them on his muddy pants. By the time he'd nerved himself to mention this, McDougal had loped off and discovered the cake of grayish-white soap sitting in a metal dish beside the hose.

"I want a cast of any footprints around the faucet."

But any footprints were lost in a muddy muck. The detective who'd been summoned to make a cast was indignant. "Leaky faucet. And somebody turned off the hose at the nozzle instead of here."

McDougal's flashlight went on probing and found a stick as long as his arm, one end thick with slime, as if it might have been used to stir a witches' cauldron. To roil the wet earth and obliterate what? It was too wet and too muddy to show fingerprints. "But take along the soap."

The detective whipped out a plasticine envelope for the soap. "Man from Glad," he said, in a revoltingly cheerful voice. McDougal, who ignored all television commercials, frowned in a baffled way and handed over the sample from his wallet. "Have the lab check on this and the cake of soap and see if they're the same."

McDougal turned to Terrizi. "Better find Mario so we can ask him a few questions."

"You mean if he's back home in bed I should get him up and

bring him in right now?" The sergeant's voice rose in a surge of anguish.

"I'll ask Waters to go instead. You look around town for the car Lowry came in. It's Miss Dilworth's—a Mercedes-Benz two-eighty—green."

"There's a green Mercedes in front of the Inn. I noticed it coming in because it was parked too far out from the curb." The sergeant saw no reason to add that in his haste to report for duty he had almost bashed the Mercedes's left rear fender. "I'll check out the license but I'm pretty sure."

McDougal sat down on the rustic bench near the steps and was lighting a cigarette. In the flare of the lighter, his face was all planes and hollows, tightly stretched over bone. "Two blocks away—that's odd. If Lowry had arranged to meet someone here and didn't want the car to be seen at the Center. . . ."

With rushing relief, the sergeant said, "He wouldn't have arranged to meet Angie's uncle."

"Stop calling him Angie's uncle. If Mario turns out to be a suspect the fact that he's Angie's uncle doesn't enter in."

Didn't enter in! It was entering in like a tidal wave, or a fox in the vitals. "Yes, sir," Terrizi said stoically.

"But Mario doesn't smell right to me as a killer. He might give somebody a push when he was drunk, but if this killing was set up the way I think it was, he's too guileless for it."

The sergeant's eyes widened. An Italian without guile? Like a woman without a mouth. But if the inspector chose to pursue this line of thought, let him, Godspeed.

An ambulance siren howled.

Below them in the garden, men had begun the grisly task of untangling Davin Lowry from "Touch Therapy."

7

Mrs. Beeton was still sprawled back side up on the inspector's bed when he went home at dawn to shower and shave. The reminder of stuffed pork was so repulsive he slammed the book shut as if he were slamming the door on a fat, greasy face.

When he raised the blinds, the room shimmered in golden light—one of those glorious, bird-twittered June mornings that in theory makes one glad to be alive, but in practice can make one feel stinking awful in contrast. McDougal felt gritty gray, and as if he were dragging along in leg chains. His earlier elation over discovering the soap on the steps had sagged into gloomy exasperation. The soap trick was too simple-minded, somehow; as a method of murder, it was ludicrously chancy. But whether it had got the right victim or the wrong one, it had worked. Remembering this, the inspector climbed into the shower with excessive caution, like a bundle of brittle old bones, and clutched the cake of Yardley's in an unyielding fist. Usually he preferred very cold showers, but today he started with water so hot that, when he plugged in his electric razor ten minutes later, the bathroom mirror was still steamed over. He had no desire to see himself face to face anyway; he shaved by touch, while his mind wandered in and out of dark alleys.

Had Davin Lowry arranged to meet somebody after the concert? A woman? Otherwise, why the devious bit about parking the Mercedes two blocks away from the Center? He'd told Grace he was going in to pick up the slides, but the slides hadn't been in his jacket pocket and they hadn't been in the Mural Room on the table beside the projector. Two state troopers had searched the garden and the vacant lot, and no slides had turned up. The only footprints identified so far, in the rain-dampened earth, were the dead man's, coming in the back way through the vacant lot, and another set of prints at the top of the steps, by a bench. So Lowry must have first gone *up* the steps, but he hadn't fallen then. At least, he'd presumably reached the top safely if he'd stood by the bench. Or had that been earlier in the day? But the rain had started before seven, and Lowry and Grace Dilworth must have gone home by then. No, she'd said, "We left everything scattered around in a mess as soon as the rain started."

McDougal got out a fresh shirt, but it felt limp as soon as he put it on. He reached absently for a tie and was knotting it before he saw it was a Cardin design his wife had given him two or three years before. For so impulsive a woman, Eileen had been surprisingly restrained in choosing his ties. He'd actually liked wearing them. He'd always trusted her taste in clothes. He thought bitterly, I trusted her, period. The great Inspector McCuckold.

Unconsciously, he'd yanked the tie so tight it felt like a noose. He ripped it off and got out a bow tie, defiantly, because Eileen had disliked bow ties; she'd said they made him look like the professor in *Little Women:* "Meek and stoop-shouldered."

McDougal put on his lightweight summer jacket, pulled back his shoulders and stood rigidly straight, as if he were a rookie cop on inspection. The thought streaked through his mind that Grace Dilworth must be almost five feet ten. Only woman he'd ever walked with who could keep pace. And good reflexes. If she hadn't grabbed me at the top of the steps when I skidded . . . one of the few things Grace had said afterward, in a sad, low voice, was, "Davin wanted to take out the stone steps and put in a ramp down to the sculpture garden. And now it's too late— the steps killed him."

It hadn't been the steps; it had been somebody who'd schemed for a coroner's verdict of accidental death. McDougal hoped that when Grace Dilworth learned it was murder, the shock of it might be therapeutic. Jolt her into anger. And that was a lot healthier than apathy. He must talk to her this afternoon. He found he wasn't dreading it at all. In fact, the thought that she'd learn of his astuteness in spotting the soap trick made him feel quite on his toes. Seven forty now. Get some breakfast and then start interviewing the others. The prospect of questioning Alec Foster and members of the board didn't give him the same invigorating sensation as he'd had when he thought of Grace.

In the kitchen, he got the can of Martinson's coffee out of the refrigerator (Lucy insisted coffee stayed fresher that way), then discovered he was out of filters for the Chemex pot. New box somewhere in a bottom cupboard; too much trouble to find it now. He had meant to open it last evening, but then he'd had dinner with Lucy. Have to watch out for Lucy's blind spots on this case. Where Foster and Melton were concerned, she'd be like a lioness protecting her newly adopted cubs. Better not say too much to her right now. Just stop and see her briefly on the way out, around eight thirty.

The leftover frozen orange juice tasted tinny, and he took only a few swallows before he poured the rest down the drain. He eased two eggs into boiling water and both of them cracked instantly. Globules of slippery white albumen floated to the surface like dead fish, and the sight took away whatever small appetite he had. To hell with it. He wouldn't even make toast. He overheaped a teaspoon with instant coffee, put it into a cup, and was tilting the kettle of boiling water when something whacked sharply against the front door. Boiling water spurted onto the drainboard and cascaded over the floor. It didn't actually splash on him, but it scalded his already raw nerve ends, and he cursed savagely.

The peculiar noise continued. Not pounding or knocking. More as if somebody were trying to kick the door in. He looked out the kitchen window and caught a glimpse of Lucy's curly white hair.

Of all the brassy nerve. Lucy was actually trying to kick his door in like an FBI agent on television. Not even bothering to ring the bell. He strode into the living room, and by the time he slid the bolt and got the front door open, he was seething with inhospitality. "What the—" he began, when his vocal cords were knotted by the sight of Lucy balancing a huge tray covered with a white napkin.

"About time," she said. "Take this before I drop it. I heard you come home and I thought you'd be too done in to get breakfast. I didn't want to eat alone anyway. Grace is still doped. What a horrible thing. Don't just stand there holding it. Over there."

McDougal, still speechless, put the tray on the trestle table under the big north window.

"Get cups and plates while I take things out. If there's anything I loathe, it's cold, congealed food."

The kippered herrings were hot and of rousing flavor. So were the scrambled eggs. The coffee came steaming, richly black, from a thermos pitcher. "Don't tell me any details till you've finished. First you eat. I sound like a Jewish mother in books. If I'd given birth at the age of six, I could be your mother. But six is young, even for India. Oh, I nearly forgot the—" She reached for a drawstring bag that reminded McDougal of the reticule his Scots grandmother had carried around to hold her steel-rimmed spectacles, knitting, and peppermints shaped like tiny pillows, with soft centers. Lucy's reticule, when she pulled it open, produced not peppermints but something the size of a brick wrapped in silver foil. "Apple spice bread. Get a board, will you, and a knife? I couldn't sleep, so I baked up a batch around six. It's supposed to have walnuts in it, but I didn't have any walnuts and I think they'd be too much, anyway, with the kippered herrings."

She took a bite, said "Mmmm" with satisfaction, and picked up her fork. They ate in the intent silence of people who've been without food for days. After ten minutes and a third cup of coffee, McDougal felt as if he'd had a good long nap, or a slap-up stay in a sauna.

"I know we had a gentlemen's agreement not to drop in on each other, but I thought if I phoned you and said I'd bring breakfast over, you'd say no. And I couldn't ask you to come to the house because I want Grace to sleep as long as she can. Of course I didn't ask her any questions last night. All I know is, he fell. I put the electric blanket on high when I got her to bed, and by the time I turned it down she was already dead to the world." Hearing her own words, she winced. "But poor Davin Lowry's dead to the world forever. Those damn steps have been a menace for years. The only way I'd go down them now is on hands and knees backward. The policeman who brought Grace here said he thought it was a broken neck."

McDougal gave silent credit to the cop who'd given so considerate a version in the middle of the night. He could imagine the reasoning: fragile little white-haired widow lady—mustn't shock her too bad. Maybe at 3 A.M. I'd have told her the same thing.

But in the strong north light from the window, with Lucy looking straight at him, equivocation stuck in his gullet. The problem was how much to tell.

"You look as if you're sitting on something and can't decide whether to hatch."

The inspector hatched—to a degree. He told her about the two pieces of sculpture flanking the steps at the bottom. "Lowry fell against one of them and was killed instantly."

Lucy said sadly, "He set up his own Scylla and Charybdis. It's as if the Fates had to punish him. But he didn't deserve this. He and Grace were so excited and happy. They weren't thinking of anybody else's feelings, but people in love don't know anybody else *has* feelings. They weren't ruthless deliberately, they were just double-minded—only the two of them mattered." She stopped, then repeated slowly, "Double-minded. It's odd I said that. I meant single-minded. When Davin phoned here last night, I had a feeling that—well, it doesn't matter now. The thing that haunts me is that I didn't let him come over and talk. I was tired and bad-tempered—he'd put us all in a bad temper at that meeting—especially Alec. He and Alec hackled their back hairs from the minute they met. It was one reason I wondered. . . ." She shook the thermos pitcher, heard it gurgle, and said in a hostess-y tone, "How about more coffee?"

70

McDougal shook his head. "You wondered what?"

"Oh, nothing important." She picked up her fork again and pursued a fragment of scrambled egg with elaborate concern.

"Tell me anyway." He hadn't meant to sound so terse.

"I dislike that third-degree manner of yours. But if you must know, I simply wondered if Davin and Alec would work well together."

"That's not what you started to say."

Lucy said vehemently, "He's dead and I refuse to play unpleasant guessing games. If I knew something positive, I'd tell you. But I don't know a thing for sure except that he and Grace were going to be married. And I'm heartsick for her. I'm so thankful you drove her in last night. Imagine if she'd found Davin by herself. I can't bear to think of it. What a hideous, senseless accident."

Now it was the inspector's turn to stall. He made a great production of putting out his cigarette, poking at an imaginary last spark.

Lucy said sharply, "It *was* an accident, wasn't it?"

"Nothing's been decided officially."

"But you think it was murder. Why? Those steps were insanely steep—it's a miracle nobody's been killed there before. If it's because I told you last night we were all furious at Davin—that's ridiculous. I was just worked up. I don't usually go off the deep end like that."

McDougal suppressed a snort.

"I gave you the wrong impression entirely. We weren't in a rage. We were—well, fuming because we wanted that parking lot. But I really liked the man. We hit it off right away. That's why he wanted to talk to me privately, and if he was murdered, I feel guiltier than ever."

"Now who's being ridiculous? It wasn't your fault in the least. Unless you killed him so you could pair Grace off with somebody else."

"That's a disgusting remark."

"It was supposed to be a joke. But if the shoe pinches. . . ."

Lucy looked a bit flustered. "Of *course* I'm not thinking of any such thing, when the poor man hasn't even been buried yet. I do hope Grace won't let that minister talk her into a long-drawn-out service. Sam Dilworth gave so much money to the church, and the minister is the hearty young extrovert sort who loves to put on a show. So did Sam, for that matter; he'd have adored his own funeral. Like an island chieftain's—the waving-plumes panoply. Grace went through all that hoopla when he died and she stood up remarkably well. She has guts, that girl."

McDougal said, more to himself, "She needed them last night."

"I think I'll keep her here a few weeks, so she won't feel so alone. We could cheer her up at meals and play gin rummy or something in the evenings."

McDougal gave her a suspicious look, and Lucy fell back on Clausewitz's theory—the best defense is attack. She said fiercely, "Hasn't Grace been through enough, without your opening up a hornet's nest of murder investigation?"

"I can't sweep evidence under the rug just because you women want everything tidy."

"What evidence?"

McDougal said childishly, "If you hold out on me about why Lowry wanted to see you, then I'll hold out on you."

"But I'm not holding out." Lucy opened her dark blue eyes very wide. "Truly. I just didn't think you wanted me to subject you to Woman's Intuition."

"It wouldn't affect my own judgment."

"Of all the stolid male arrogance. I'm damned if I'll tell you a thing." She got up and began stacking the tray with angry bangs and clatter. "You didn't even say thank you for breakfast."

It had been churlish not to say thank you; the breakfast had been fork-to-mouth resuscitation. But now the inspector couldn't bring himself to admit it. "I had a lot on my mind."

"Who hasn't? That's no excuse for abominable manners." She marched to the door. "You may leave the tray at my kitchen door. And after this, when you're hungry, you may open a can of worms."

She had her hand on the knob when McDougal capitulated: "The steps were soaped."

Lucy whirled around. "Mac!" She clutched at her chest as if the news had stabbed her physically. "But was it meant for Davin? With the concert last night, anybody could have gone out and fallen. . . ."

"I nearly did myself. Grace caught my arm just in time."

"Grace saved your life!"

This was a slight exaggeration, but Lucy seemed so buoyed by the thought he let it pass. She came back and sat down and propped her chin on her hands expectantly, waiting. McDougal had always thought it was a simperingly affected pose in women, but with Lucy it wasn't affected; it was a sign of so vivid and total an interest that even men who started with a mouthful of pebbles had been known to spill out like a landslide.

The inspector didn't go to blabbing extremes, but he told her more than he'd originally intended, partly because it was such a flattering change to have Lucy doing the listening. "And after we'd sent the soap to the lab, we found Mario back of his greenhouse, in his truck. He'd passed out cold."

Lucy reverted to her normal role of doing the talking: "Mario wouldn't hurt a flea. Though as a matter of fact, he would. He caught fleas one time from sleeping with his dog and he was jumping around and twitching as if he had Saint Vitus's dance. So that's not a good simile, but it's the sentiment that counts. Mario wouldn't trample on a flower, let alone kill a man."

"This man was out to wreck his rose garden."

Lucy made a sound that was almost a whimper. "If I'd let Davin come over here last evening, I might have talked him out of it."

"But that's not what you thought Lowry wanted to talk to you about."

"N-n-no. I think it was something about getting married. I don't mean he wasn't crazy about Grace. He was." A slight touch of cunning slid into her voice. "Why wouldn't he be?" She was pleased that her listener didn't refute this. "And Grace has enough money to do whatever she and a husband might feel like. With inflation and food prices and everything, that's an added attraction. But Davin didn't care about her money."

McDougal's long, bony face expressed a dour skepticism.

"Really. He told me that and he meant it. I know he was telling the truth."

"A walking lie detector." He knew it was a bad remark as soon as he'd said it. All the more because he had real respect for Lucy's perceptions, more than he had for lie detectors. He couldn't have put this into words; it would have been what he thought of as "smarmy." And there wasn't time anyway. He'd lit a short fuse and Lucy was already exploding.

"Unlike you, I care about people, and so they want to confide in me. Your lack of warmth and understanding must be a big handicap in police work—and in all human relationships."

She'd jabbed where it hurt, and he jabbed back on reflex. "You mean I ought to have the woman's touch, but unfortunately I'm not a homo. That reminds me, I'd better catch Alec Foster before he goes in to the Center. If he and Lowry were hostile to each other from the start, then he might have been afraid Lowry would fire him or get Grace to do it. So Foster would have a motive."

"It was *not* that kind of hostility. It wasn't murderous, it was petulant."

Odd word for her to choose—*petulant*. Even talking off the top of her head, to defend a friend, it was curiously revealing. "Do you mean because they disagreed on art?"

Lucy said too quickly, "Yes, that was it. But Davin had absolutely no interest in taking Alec's job. In a way, it was Fred Thorndike he was replacing. Fred adores Grace, and he'd wanted to do the parking lot just to please her as a memorial to her father. Oh, maybe now we can still have the parking place."

"And Fred Thorndike will have Grace? How convenient." And not at all welcome a notion. McDougal decided crossly he would put Thorndike up top on the list of possible suspects.

"Fred's not enough of a man for Grace. She needs somebody stronger." Lucy's gaze flittered innocently past the inspector to the front window, as if savoring the scenery. "Oh, here's Nicky." She raised her voice. "Come in, dear. Would you like a kippered herring that's slightly cold?"

"No, ma'am. I wouldn't even like one hot. I mean, I already ate at Angie's." Whatever he'd eaten couldn't have sat well. The young sergeant's terra-cotta coloring was tinged with saffron hue. "When I went to tell them Mario's in jail."

"In jail! Mac, did you know they put Mario in jail?"

He not only knew it, he had ordered it done, and he'd carefully refrained from mentioning it earlier. A dignified nod was all he'd allow himself now.

"I never heard of anything so outrageous."

"It's not as outrageous as murder."

"What's that got to do with it? You know very well Mario would never plan a clever way to kill somebody."

The inspector was inclined to the same opinion. Anybody who would attack a cop with a rosebush was too Mack-Sennett-comedy to be crafty. "For the moment, I want him in protective custody."

"If you throw an innocent man in jail, then at least have the decency to stop calling it by fancy names. Protective custody, my foot. What if he hanged himself? He's never liked being indoors. Nicky dear, how awful for you—Angie's favorite uncle."

Terrizi regarded his new ally gratefully. "Angie's mama is so sore at the police she says the wedding is off. She says maybe three years from now."

"But that's inhuman. What does she think you're made of—saltpeter? Why don't you tell Angie's mother that if she postpones the wedding, you'll sleep together? Of course, you probably already have, but if you threatened to do it publicly, I don't mean in Macy's window but living together openly—then she'd have to give in."

The sergeant hunched his shoulders, shrinking into himself, and his head rolled back and forth, indicating a certain apprehension.

"Then why not elope? That's nice and old-fashioned."

"Angie wouldn't do it. She loves her mama."

"Strange taste. I know what that woman's like. She used to work for Hal and me years ago, and she's quite a good cook—she did one or two dishes better even than I do—but once I caught her cleaning the silver coffeepot with steel wool, and when she's criticized she goes off like a geyser, shooting in all directions."

The two men looked at each other, communicating wordlessly: Look who's talking.

"It's not fair for her to penalize you and Angie. Tell her it's all Mac's fault for making a stupid mistake."

The sergeant said miserably, "The evidence pointed at Mario."

"Then it's a plant. Mario simply doesn't have the temperament for that sort of thing. Let's think who does. Myra Farmington, for one. She's a very vindictive, neurotic woman. And I don't mean just normal neurotic. Once when she wanted to be chairman of the Thrift Shop's annual bazaar, the committee chose me instead because I have taste and they knew I'd decorate the place well. And Myra was wild. She thinks of herself as 'old family' and she acted as if we'd desecrated the Farmington ancestral totem pole. She wrote me the weirdest anonymous letter, saying I thought I was so 'artistic'—poor Davin Lowry, he loathed that word too. She probably saw us nudging each other and making faces when George used it at the meeting. Anyway, she said in the letter I didn't have the 'hands of an artistic person'—that my fingers were stubby like a peasant's." Lucy spread out her square, small, capable hands on the table and regarded them critically. "She was right, too. But I'd rather have a good healthy streak of peasant blood than that lower-middle-class minciness of hers. And talons! When she was George's secretary, she wore her nails so long she had to claw at the typewriter keys. She must have clawed even harder when she was typing that anonymous letter."

McDougal had been interested from the mention of "vindictive," because it sounded like a lead. But now he was puzzled. "If the letter was typed and unsigned, how did you know she wrote it?"

"It stank of her perfume," Lucy said triumphantly. "And my sense of smell is as good as my hearing. Like a cat's. But I never told her I knew. Hal and I did the most smashing decorations for the Thrift Shop bazaar Wingate has ever seen. Arabian Nights murals. They were so enchanting that people who came to buy the usual homemade doodads like potholders and aprons insisted on buying our decorations." She glowed, remembering. "The bazaar made a huge amount of money. And Myra's hated me ever since. And she was so outraged at Davin yesterday she tried to walk out of the meeting, but George wouldn't let her. She's definitely killer material."

Sergeant Terrizi was visibly cheered to have Myra Farmington's head offered on a platter instead of Mario's. And he was emboldened to add an alternative head: "If you ask me, Grace Dilworth is killer material, too."

He was too intent to notice the expressions of his listeners: first surprise, then tolerant amusement. "The way she used to shoot the heads off marigolds."

"Oh, that was just when Sam gave her a new twenty-two and she wanted to practice and show him how good she was."

"She was too good," Terrizi said grimly.

The inspector exercised patience. "Lowry wasn't shot. The pathologist checked on that first—at my request. And remember I saw Grace Dilworth in her upstairs window *after* the car drove away."

"The Mercedes drove away. But they've always had two cars."

"Not any more. Grace sold Sam's Cadillac, that big black hearse thing, before she left on the cruise. Nicky dear, I can understand why you want to clear Mario—we all do—but Grace *loved* Davin Lowry. She was going to marry him."

"They always suspect the husband or wife first." The sergeant was hanging onto his theory like a puppy clenching a bone.

"But they weren't even married yet. So that's out." Lucy sat back as if on her own climax.

McDougal felt paternally concerned; the boy was talking too wildly. "I want you to go home and get some sleep, and then you'll see things more in perspective. You've had a bad night."

"Today's worse," the sergeant said broodingly. "And I couldn't sleep anyway. I want to get to work and help crack this case. Who are we going to interview first?"

The inspector had already made up his mind that Terrizi wasn't to interview anybody at this point. Let the sergeant keep busy on something more drudging than diplomatic. "We'll have to identify the casts of all the footprints. You can go around this morning and collect a shoe from—say—each one of the board members, to start with. Use the 'just routine investigation' line."

Terrizi looked less than enthusiastic. Lucy said, "It's too bad you don't have a shoe fetish, so you'd enjoy the job more."

"Get a shoe from Alec Foster too. And while you're about it, get one from his 'dearest friend' Melton." Lucy glared at him, and the inspector added hurriedly, "We aren't playing any favorites. Check on Miss Dilworth's."

Lucy said, "I will not have Grace wake up and find her shoes gone. You can get another shoe from her maid. Her feet are much bigger than the rest of ours, so her prints will be unmistakable."

McDougal yielded. "We don't have to check whether there's mud on hers anyway, because we know she was in the rose garden at two A.M. But get one of Mario's."

"If I asked Angie or her mama for one of Mario's shoes, they'd throw it at me."

"Doesn't Mario have his shoes on in jail?" Lucy asked. "I think you *both* need some sleep."

But Sergeant Terrizi's eyes were suddenly bright with purposeful resolve. He had thought of a detective project of his own.

8

The huge forsythia bush to the left of the Dilworth driveway looked blowsily fat but with bald patches, like a woman who's gone to seed. Sergeant Terrizi, even in his preoccupied state, noticed this as he drove in and felt the born gardener's pang over neglect. Should have been pruned last summer. He remembered when Mario had rescued it from the grounds of an old house being razed for a development. They'd borrowed a crane to lift the mammoth thing out, and it had been like transplanting an elephant with a dozen dangling trunks. Mario had done all the Dilworths' gardening in those days, and he'd been strutting proud of the forsythia when he'd finally anchored it where he felt it belonged.

But the Dilworths, father and daughter, hadn't even commented on the spectacular acquisition. Mario had said to his fifteen-year-old helper, "It's like instant coffee—their kind expects instant flowers." Sergeant Terrizi felt a scornful superiority, remembering this, but as he drove nearer the massive, imposingly ugly stone house, the superiority crumbled under an upsurge of the long-ago nervousness of that fifteen-year-old.

He half expected Sam Dilworth, with his jutting jaw, to stomp out and bellow, "What the hell you doing, parking in the front drive? Get around to the back where you belong." There was a separate driveway to the rear with a sign on the gatepost: SERVICE ENTRANCE, and he had always come in that way on foot or in Mario's truck. You're here on official business, he told himself. You park right in front and you push the front doorbell and when the housekeeper comes you say "Police" and show your identification. But the palms of his hands were sweating when he gave the bell a small, tentative poke.

He expected to see the stout, middle-aged housekeeper who had bawled him out once for using the bathroom off the basement laundry and "dirtying the soap." He stood very stiff and straight, clutching his ID card, ready to face his old antagonist and stare her down. But the maid who came to the door was a young black amazon in a mini-skirted white uniform. She looked as if she'd been crying, which unnerved him, and all the more because she was pretty. He managed to deliver his prepared opening speech about official business, but the girl was already spilling out words.

"Mrs. Ramsdale came over and told me as soon as I got here this morning. It's terrible—I still can't believe it. I'm getting some of Miss Grace's clothes together now. You want I should give you the suitcases?"

He blurted out, "I just want one of her shoes."

"How come you don't want two shoes? She hurt her foot?"

The sergeant mumbled something about "routine investigation . . . footprints . . . if you'd just let me look in her closet and pick something. I'm sorry to bother you."

"No bother." Actually, it sounded more like "nuh botha," and her lilting accent reminded him of his colleague on the Wingate police force who had come from Jamaica. He said on impulse, "You know Sergeant Bayles?"

The maid's face shone with pleasure. "His sister's my best girl friend."

After that, it was pie. The girl led him upstairs, and he had time to notice that her legs were good, but not as good as Angie's, when she opened a door on the left. She rushed into the room first, smoothed the ivory damask spread on the bed, then flung open the double closet doors while the sergeant was still paralyzed on the threshold, terrified to step on the virginally white nylon carpeting.

"Pay it no nevermind," the maid said hospitably. "I got one of those electric carpet-shampoo things. Miss Grace tracks in dirt all the time."

As Terrizi tiptoed across the velvety, deep-piled white expanse, all he saw was a large, silver-framed photograph of Grace's father in riding clothes, holding a crop, watching him from the dressing table. The sight didn't add to his nonchalance.

The maid was gesturing at the shoe racks on the back of both doors. There were perhaps two dozen pairs of shoes, most of them sensible, low-heeled oxfords and loafers in white, tan, and brown, but on the top row on one side, like a late-flowering bloom, there were the giddy high-heeled pumps, greens and blues and gold. "Poor, poor lady. She just getting used to dressing pretty for her boyfriend, then he falls down dead. You knew him —her Mr. Lowry?"

Terrizi shook his head.

"Nicest man you'd want to meet. And neat! He never left so much as a handkerchief laying around. And whenever he took a shower, he put that ole towel right back on the rack, folded nice, even while it was wet."

The sergeant thought sourly, Mama would have loved him.

"Him and Miss Grace were a couple of lovebirds. Talking sugar talk morning, noon and night."

It wasn't at all what the sergeant wanted to hear, and unconsciously he grimaced.

"You don't believe they were sweet?" Now she was the young warrior maiden waving a spear. "You're wrong, man. Never saw two people so crazy about one another. Holding hands all over the place—don't care who sees 'em. Miss Grace kept looking at him like she'd eat him with a spoon. This will break her heart worse'n a china plate hit with an ax. First her daddy, then her man."

To cut short this unwelcome talk—unwelcome because it tore holes in the case he was trying to weave out of bits and pieces like a bird's nest—the sergeant picked out one of the shoes at random, a tan leather loafer with a steel buckle.

Now he had to broach something that wasn't strictly official business, more Terrizi sticking his nose in, looking for he wasn't sure what. He said, "Which room did Mr. Lowry have?"

The maid waved to the closed door directly across the hall. "Gillian—Sergeant Bayles—already told me to keep it locked till Detective Waters gets here."

So that settled that. The girl saw him droop. "You want I should call Gillie at the police station and ask if it's all right to let you in?"

To be uncovered as a snoop who exceeded orders for personal reasons . . . the sergeant's "No" was almost a shout.

As they left the room, the maid glanced at the locked door across the hall, and her face crinkled with merriment. "That was Mr. Lowry's room, but he sure didn't use the bed much." As if to stress, belatedly, the legitimate aspects, she said quickly, "You know, they were going to be married. Miss Grace told me herself last night when they got home from some meeting. I told her I'd stay to serve dinner, but she said, 'We want to take our time, Zora. Bring up a bottle of champagne and glasses.' They kept champagne in the icebox all the time the way you and me would keep Pepsi. Then Mr. Lowry told me to bring another glass so I could drink to their happiness. But I only poured me a litty-bitty sip because I don't like champagne. It tastes like when you're swimmin' and you get water up your nose. The two of them emptied the bottle, though."

The sergeant thought wishfully, Maybe Miss Dilworth got Lowry drunk so he'd go fall down those steps. Maybe she doped his champagne. Terrizi was careful not to ask himself why a woman should dope her adored fiancé and then let him go off to the soap-slicked steps to take a fatal tumble. "Have you still got the glasses they drank out of?"

"Of course we got 'em. You think they're like paper cups, to throw in the trash bin? Those glasses are in the dishwasher, where Mr. Lowry put 'em last night. He was real good about cleaning up after supper. Miss Grace used to just let the dishes and stuff sit on the table, but he'd rinse 'em and stack 'em in the dishwasher every night. I was sure looking forward to him living here full time as a husband."

The sergeant was still doggedly pursuing his unlikely premise. "Has the dishwasher been run yet?"

"Chuggin' away right now."

So that was another lost lead. And Detective Waters was to look through the dead man's possessions. But there was another place Detective Waters wouldn't have been told to look, and it was the crux of the sergeant's theory. "I'll just go out through the kitchen door. Is the bicycle still kept in the garage?"

"What bicycle?" Zora asked. "Miss Grace and her daddy both had bikes, but she was so upset when he died she didn't want 'em around any more. Like his car, only she sold that. The bikes she just gave away. She asked me if I'd like one. Would I like one! English—real fancy."

"What happened to the other one?"

"She gave it to some friend."

He made one more try. "You didn't happen to leave yours here last night?"

"Why should I leave it here? I got my own car. It's parked out in back." She waved toward a window. "But Gillie Bayles and his sister and me—we go bike-riding most every Sunday. Folks come from Jamaica, they're practically born on a bicycle." She was off, talking very fast and liltingly about the unpolluted pleasures of cycling in Ocho Rios as compared to the hazards of Connecticut roads, but her listener was drearily uninterested. His dream of glory—telling the inspector he'd found the bicycle Grace rode into town, with the mud from the rose garden still on it— was in tatters. All he had left to go on was one of her shoes, but his feelings were hardly those of the prince: he didn't want a happy ending for Cinderella.

"One shoe won't do her much good," the maid said as he was leaving. "She needs dresses and nighties and a toothbrush. Mrs. Ramsdale wants to keep her there for a week or two. And when Miss Grace wakes up today, she won't want to put on those clothes she was wearing when she found him dead. How come he fell down anyway? He was a mighty athletic young man. Swimmin' in the pool, playin' tennis—you know, we got lovely tennis courts in Jamaica now. Brand-new. Mr. Lowry was talking to me about it. And Miss Grace said they ought to go to my island on their honeymoon, but he didn't seem to care for that much."

The idea of being able to have any honeymoon, even a night in a motel without Angie's mama hexing, seemed to the young sergeant bliss beyond all other promises of Paradise. And for a man to turn down Jamaica—blasé bastard. He was glad to have another reason for disliking the dead man, beyond the fact that his death had ruined Terrizi's love life. "You mean he and Miss Dilworth were fighting about where to go on their honeymoon?"

"Them two fight? She'd do anything he'd a mind to. Last thing I heard her tell him, laughing, was that they could spend their wedding night with the lost wife, looking civilized."

This unexpected tidbit elated the sergeant. If Lowry had had a wife who turned up out of the blue after Grace Dilworth thought he was divorced. . . . But, in that case, why had Grace been so good-humored, laughing and suggesting they spend a honeymoon with the woman? The sergeant had heard of couples being "civilized" after a divorce, but this triangular form of being civilized congealed his Latin blood. What hotted it up again was the realization that he had a sizzling bit of inside news, after all, to take to the inspector. Because if Grace Dilworth had talked amiably about getting together with an ex-wife in a civilized fashion, and then had caught Lowry having a sneak rendezvous with the woman in the rose garden, and turned savage. . . . Maybe she'd soaped the steps to catch the wife and caught her lover instead. That made real sense.

He elaborated on this theme so convincingly to himself that it seemed imperative to rush the good news to State Police Barracks A, on the other side of Wingate, where Inspector McDougal had gone to read lab reports. First, he had to finish his collect-a-shoe stint. He had already got one from Flora Pollit, an arch-support model with a rubber heel, and had had to stem her flow of propaganda: if people wore shoes they could walk miles in, they wouldn't pollute the atmosphere or weaken the muscles God gave them For a Purpose. Flora had even implied that people who wore the right shoes would never be so feckless as to fall down a flight of stone steps.

Following the inspector's instructions, Terrizi hadn't mentioned murder. So far, it was "accidental death," and they were "merely checking for footprints of possible witnesses to the tragedy." Alec Foster's assistant, Martha Teague, whom he caught as she was leaving for the Center, had accepted this fuzzy explanation, or seemed to, but with less chatter than Flora, and had turned over a flat-heeled sandal with braided thongs.

Myra Farmington said the sergeant's request was an outrageous invasion of privacy; she had drawn herself up *grande-dame*-ly, as if the sergeant were asking for a souvenir bra and panties. George Farmington had come from the breakfast table, napkin in hand and a dab of egg yolk on his thin upper lip, to override his wife's hoity refusal.

"We want to cooperate with the authorities in every possible way. A terrible thing, this accident. Sad for Miss Dilworth, and for all of us who met Mr. Lowry and heard his—uh—stimulating ideas."

Terrizi thought, He's laying it on like a funeral wreath while he's chortling inside. Because of Lucy's description of Myra Farmington as a vindictive sort, the sergeant was tempted to ask, Where were you last night between ten and twelve? But he didn't have the nerve to ask her right out; he waited till she'd gone, reluctantly, to collect the shoes, and then asked her husband.

George Farmington put his napkin to his lips (as if he were going to spit something out?) and then said, "Mrs. Farmington and I were at the concert, of course. We support all cultural activities at the Center. And afterward we went backstage to pay our respects to the pianist, a most talented *artiste*. Alec Foster should have been responsible for taking her back to the Inn, but he said he had some chores to do first in the office, so rather than allow her to be kept waiting, we drove her there ourselves. We were home by eleven." As his wife reappeared, he said, "Isn't that so, my dear? I've just been saying we were home by eleven."

Myra snapped, "I can't see that it's any of this boy's business."

"Myra! He represents the law."

Myra's sniff implied that the majesty of the law had shrunk pitifully, to descend to the likes of Terrizi, but she confirmed her husband's account. "And make sure you return these shoes by tomorrow—in good condition."

The sergeant thought of what he'd like to put in her shoe, but he only said woodenly, "Yes, ma'am," and got out of there fast.

He had already gone to Alec Foster's place on his way to Grace Dilworth's. Nobody home. Now he stopped at Fred Thorndike's and was rather relieved to have silence greet his thumping of the brass knocker. He'd ask a state trooper to collect the other shoes later that morning. He, Terrizi, had something much better than shoes to bring the inspector.

He found McDougal in the back office of Barracks A, reading a teletype report, and he told what he'd learned from the maid. He was eagerly ready to go on and explain his newest theory the second he was encouraged, but McDougal was repeating in a bemused voice, "Honeymoon with the lost wife, looking civilized." His eyebrows went up, hovered in thought, then descended fast. His long, bony face began to broaden into a grin, but he controlled himself in time.

"It's the other statue—'Lot's Wife Looking at Civilization.' Miss Dilworth was joking about Lowry's being so wrapped up in the sculpture garden."

Terrizi tried desperately to salvage something from the debris: "But if Lowry didn't want to go on a honeymoon—maybe he wanted to postpone the marriage because he knew he still had a wife."

The inspector held up the teletype. "The police on the West Coast have no record of a Davin Lowry ever taking out a marriage license." He read aloud, skimming. ". . . lived with his mother in Pasadena until her death four years ago . . . bachelor apartment afterward . . . last job, curator of a small sculpture museum . . . took a leave from his job to travel . . . had inherited money from his mother. . . ." He put the teletype sheet into a manila folder labeled LOWRY. "Lucy said Lowry wasn't after the Dilworth money, and this sounds as if she's right."

"She usually is," the sergeant said, with dejection. He stared into space, as if into an endless black tunnel full of scuttling rats. But then his dark eyes livened. "If she thinks Mario's innocent, she's apt to be right."

"Lucy's friends are always O.K. On Judgment Day, she'll sit at the Devil's right hand and keep saying, 'Oh, you wouldn't want *him*—he's a friend of mine. Let me take him back upstairs where it's cooler.'"

Terrizi was not amused. He looked, if anything, gloomier, and his mood was contagious. McDougal had become more accustomed than he knew to the young sergeant's responsive, admiring attitudes in the role of assistant, and this sudden absence of rapport was depressing. Moreover, McDougal knew that what he had to say next would make the gap worse. He glanced at his ashtray, counted the butts—five, one over his quota for mornings, and he'd been chain-smoking all night; but this was an exception because he hadn't had any sleep. . . . He lit a fresh cigarette.

"I talked to Mario a half hour ago in the jail. He says he doesn't know anything about the soap. He admits he went back to the Arts Center last night, but we already knew that. A woman who lives in the block above the Center remembers seeing his truck parked there while the concert was going on. Yellow panel truck with black letters—she's positive. She says Mario often went to the Center at night to talk to his plants, to sing them to sleep or something. She says Mario told her once that plants need to feel loved, and they need to be talked to. She had a cactus plant that was doing poorly, but now she talks to it every day and it's flourishing. She thinks Mario is a great gardener and that the rose garden is 'one of the beauties of our town.'"

"It is," the sergeant said bitterly. "And if Miss Dilworth had had any sense. . . . But her sort doesn't care if they push people around. They don't know how to compromise. They don't even know how to say 'Please.'"

McDougal, remembering Grace's humble thank-yous to him the night before, said rather sharply, "It's true she riled people up at the meeting, but that's hardly an excuse for somebody to murder her fiancé. Mario's story is that he only went back to the garden to dig up more rosebushes, but the concert was just ending and there were too many people, so instead he went off and bought a quart of bourbon and got drunk again. The clerk in the liquor store next to Coleman's Market says Mario came in just before ten thirty. The clerk is sure because he'd already locked the door a couple of minutes before closing time, to count his cash. He'd had two holdups, so he didn't want to open up unless it was somebody he knew. He knew Mario."

"He'd know Mario like a brother," the sergeant agreed. "One of his steadiest customers."

"Or unsteadiest."

"But that's a good alibi, timewise."

"If they taught you to say 'timewise' when you took that special crime course in Stamford, then the instructor is corrupting our youth. It affects me the way the word 'artistic' affected Davin Lowry."

"But Lowry *was* artistic. So what's he kicking about? I mean, what was he kicking about?" The ugly image of Davin Lowry impaled by death thrust into the sergeant's mind; had the man tried to kick himself free, like a lynching victim? It didn't bear thinking about. Anyway, it wasn't constructive thinking. He made a mental note to avoid "timewise" before he proceeded with his thesis: "Mario couldn't have killed him and got to the liquor store by ten thirty because you said Lowry didn't even leave Miss Dilworth's to go into town till almost ten fifteen."

"Mario could have taken his quart of bourbon back to the garden. And I think he did. Because Mario was wearing boots, and his prints are imposed over Lowry's footprints, in the damp earth at the bottom of the steps. So he could have soaped the top steps and then gone down afterward to make sure his victim was dead."

The sergeant moaned like an animal in pain.

"Until he comes up with some good explanation of those footprints, we'll have to hold him. I told him again he was entitled to a lawyer, but he said next to cops he hates lawyers."

The sergeant groaned again. "He sued George Farmington because George wouldn't pay him for a job he'd done. Mrs. Farmington had wanted a Japanese rock garden to reflect 'the lovely Japanese spirit of harmony and serenity.' That's what she kept saying. And she was sore because Mario arranged the rocks so they spelled 'Remember Pearl Harbor.'"

The inspector grinned. "As an ex-Navy man, I applaud his spirit. In fact, I wish I'd been his lawyer." He began to wish he could still be Mario's lawyer. His ex-wife had said he always wanted "to swim upstream even after the mating season's over." On the face of it, Mario was the logical Number One suspect so far, but McDougal felt a renewed urge to throw logic over his left shoulder and find somebody who had made Mario Sandini the patsy. Sandini, in his cop-hating, hungover state, had been annoying and frustrating that morning in the jail. McDougal, prickly with failure, thought now, I should have kept my temper and persuaded him to talk. Maybe somebody sent him down to the rose garden on an errand when he was drunk. He started to say to Terrizi, "Why don't we—?" when a trooper appeared in the doorway. "Yes, Bowser?"

"I still can't locate Mr. Thorndike, sir. And Mr. Foster left for Kennedy Airport early this morning." His listeners gaped. "Just to put the concert pianist on a plane, sir. Mr. Foster picked up the lady at the Inn around seven thirty, and her plane leaves at ten fifteen—right about now."

"Page Mr. Alec Foster at Kennedy and ask him to call me as soon as he returns. And Bowser, make sure he does return. Have a car on his tail."

"Yes, sir." The tall trooper didn't actually salute, but his heels clicked together smartly. "I already gave those instructions."

"Good man."

The sergeant felt growlingly jealous at this praise of another. He had hoped to merit it himself, with his brilliant detection, but instead he'd bumbled into one blind alley after another.

"Mr. Foster's roommate is back at their house," Bowser said. "He says he was out marketing and he'd be glad to see you now, but he has to go to the antiques store and open it at eleven thirty."

"Tell Mr. Melton I'm on my way." The inspector reached for his cigarettes and lighter.

As McDougal got up, Terrizi leaped too. "I'll come with you." He would still do some brilliant detecting; he would help spot the guilt of Foster or Thorndike or any other suspect so long as it wasn't Angie's uncle.

McDougal shook his head. "No. I won't need you."

The sergeant slunk back to his seat like a whipped cur. To be rejected in Bowser's hearing made it even more humiliating.

"Because I want you to do something more important for me."

Beautiful, revivifying words. Terrizi leaned forward, ready to spring into action, on the balls of his feet.

"Will you pick up Angie and take her in to see Mario? Maybe he'd talk to her."

"Anybody would talk to Angie," the sergeant said joyfully.

9

It was a plain beige, canvasy cotton apron edged in brown tape. Nothing frilly or feminine. But to see it tied around Bert Melton's plump middle struck Inspector McDougal as ludicrous and even embarrassing. Obviously, Melton didn't feel that way: "I'm just fixing a cold cucumber soup for lunch. Have you ever tried doing it with farina?"

"I don't cook," McDougal said forbiddingly.

"Oh, I thought Lucy said you were quite an expert on food. Sit over here by the window." He bustled ahead and straightened a cushion. "Let's see, you smoke, don't you? Brave man. I keep the ashtrays hidden away because Alec gave it up four months ago but he still has withdrawal symptoms." He brought out a kidney-shaped white pottery piece blobbed with cerise. "Sorry the place is in such a mess outside. Alec and I are laying a terrace, and it's given me new respect for bricklayers. Really an art. I'll be with you as soon as I put the soup in to chill."

McDougal, looking out the side window at the heaped bricks and bags of sand and cement for the terrace-to-be, clustered around a wheelbarrow lying on its side, thought the mess there was preferable to the inside of the house. The back wall of the living room was painted midnight blue with silver streaks that seemed to be shooting stars on a collision course. The ceiling, a lighter, softer blue, had white clouds billowing hither and thither. A black ebony head, suspended by wire from the ceiling, dangled against the stark white wall opposite McDougal on the other side of the room. The red lacquered coffee table, at least five feet square, in front of his chair, was so squatty low he couldn't get his feet under it and had to keep his legs pulled in. Two of the lampshades were tricolored Tiffany glass—red, green, yellow—with beaded fringe. And hanging directly above one of these dreadful (to McDougal) objects was a water color that looked like Lucy's. He unwound his legs and went over to make sure. Yes—"Lucy Ramsdale" in her uphill scrawl. A scene with a carousel and children bright as flowers on the green grass. McDougal thought it was much the most attractive thing in the room.

"Charming, isn't it?" Bert Melton had come back from the kitchen, and like many big men he walked softly. He had taken off the apron and was in shirt sleeves rolled up to the elbows. His gray hair was almost as short as McDougal's, and he had a kind, broad, sensible face. His voice somehow matched it. "But the greatest thing about Lucy is her talent for living. How's she taking the news of Lowry's death? I assume that's why you're here. The janitor of the Arts Center called Alec around seven to tell him. What an incredible accident. I can't pretend—even to you, Inspector—that we were heartbroken."

McDougal could hear Sergeant Terrizi: That Bert Melton is honest as the night is long. Either Melton was being honest now, or he was giving off rays of pseudo frankness: "I never met Lowry, but he sounded like a troublemaker from what Alec told me."

"He could have been especially troublesome to Mr. Foster, I gather."

"Well, Alec wasn't taking the brunt of it like Mario Sandini. That struck me as pretty ruthless goings on, about the rose garden."

"And if he'd had Alec Foster fired, that would have been even more ruthless. After all, Lowry wasn't about to take over Sandini's job."

"That's true," Melton said quietly. "And Lowry said he didn't want Alec's job—nobody else could do the job Alec does—but he could have made life rather unpleasant. So that's why I can't weep even crocodile tears. I'm sorry for Grace, but she may have been spared a lot of unhappiness later."

"She wasn't spared any unhappiness last night around two A.M. She was with me when I found the body."

Melton looked genuinely horrified. "We didn't know that."

"And I take it you didn't know it was murder either."

Melton clasped his big hands together in a strangely girlish gesture. "Murder! Have you been able to reach Alec to tell him that?"

"I can think of one sure way he would have been the first to know."

"That's insane." His hands flew apart, protesting. "Alec would never—" But instead of sitting easily, he was hunched in his chair now, braced for more trouble.

"Were you both at the concert?"

"Yes."

"And did you return here together?"

"No, a friend drove me back. As a matter of fact, the owner of Way Back Antiques. Alec said he had to take the concert pianist back to the Inn."

"He didn't take her to the Inn. The Farmingtons told Sergeant Terrizi they drove her there themselves because Alec had something else to do."

"I must have misunderstood. But I can tell you definitely Alec was home soon after eleven. And he didn't go out again. My room's in front by the driveway, and I'd have heard the car."

"Did you go down into the rose garden any time last evening?"

"Yes. Alec had told me about the sculpture, and I went down just before the concert to take a look at the two pieces already unpacked. They were even wilder than Alec had said."

"The pronged one—'Touch Therapy'—looked especially wild with Lowry's body spiked on it."

Melton swallowed hard and put one hand on his stomach, as if trying to calm it down.

"By the way, we're checking footprints and we'll need a shoe of yours and one of Foster's. The ones you wore last night. It's a routine comparison." And it's mainly routine investigation that catches murderers. Why was it, McDougal wondered, that police used that routine bit as a reassuring phrase?

Melton didn't look reassured, but he did seem glad of an excuse to leave the room. He came back with two shoes so different in size and style that the inspector thought, Papa Bear, Mama Bear. Obviously the big brown leather oxford was Melton's; Alec's was a fawn-gray suede loafer, buckled, about the size of a woman's seven.

"I'll get you something to put those in." Melton went out to the kitchen again and brought back two plastic food-storage bags. He put one shoe in each, and fastened the top of each bag neatly with a twist tie.

"Lowry went back to the Center about ten thirty, and we think he met somebody there by appointment. Have you any reason to think it might have been Mr. Foster he was meeting?"

He saw the involuntary blink—nervousness, fear?—and then Melton said in a low, unhappy voice, "I'd rather you asked Alec that." He looked straight at the inspector. "All I can say is that if it was murder, Alec had nothing whatsoever to do with it. He abhors violence."

"Many people do—until their basic security is threatened."

"But Alec had a special reason. His youngest sister jumped out a twelfth-story window. Back in California. Alec had to identify the body, and the whole thing nearly killed him. He adored the girl. She was only twenty-three." In a totally different tone, deliberate, even calculated, he added, "She was on LSD, so of course that explains it."

McDougal, watching him, had a sense that Melton had withdrawn the frankness as suddenly as a turtle who sees danger pulls in its neck. Check with the West Coast police again. It might have been Lowry who got her on drugs. "Had Foster ever met Lowry in California?"

"Never. That I can say positively. They'd never met until yesterday."

"Or did he know anything about Lowry that would have made their first meeting hostile?"

Melton was uneasy again. He said, "That crazy sculpture would have been enough to make anybody hostile to Lowry."

It was so fey, so insulting to the listener's intelligence, that resentment overrode every other instinct in McDougal. "If you won't cooperate with the police, you and Mr. Foster may be in real trouble." As soon as he'd said it, he realized the implied threat.

So did Melton. He said steadily, "Homosexuals are used to being bullied by the police: 'Do this—tell that—betray a friend—be a stoolie or we'll throw you in jail.' But I wouldn't have expected it from you—somebody Lucy cares about and respects."

"I'm sorry if it sounded like a threat. It wasn't meant that way." But unconsciously, it was, McDougal knew, and embarrassment sat on him leadenly. With enormous effort, he made himself go on. "As a cop, I've done everything possible to see that deviants get a fair break. And the sooner they change the laws in all fifty states, the better I'll like it."

"But can they change the attitudes? You said 'deviants' just now. But deviants from whose code? As if Alec and I were freaks. When a man and woman are married, or live together, it's normal, no matter how mismated they might be. But when two homosexuals live together, at best it's something to snicker about. If I'd refused to answer your questions on the grounds that a wife can't be made to give evidence against her husband, what would you have said?"

McDougal smiled painfully. "I get your point. But I'd have said this isn't a court of law. It's a preliminary investigation. Otherwise, I'd have warned you of your rights to a lawyer, etcetera. Nobody's been accused of murder—yet. But you were so obviously evading my question: Did Foster have any reason to be hostile to Lowry from the start? And that naturally makes me think you're withholding vital evidence."

Melton spread out his hands in a rueful gesture that said, So what can I do? "I'm no good at lying. Alec should be home in another hour. And in the meantime, all I can tell you is that he would never kill anybody."

"He might not have meant to. But if, say, he tried blackmail and Lowry told him to go to hell—" Odd. McDougal realized that again he'd forgotten about the soap on the steps. *I keep thinking of a sudden violent push—not a murder plot.*

Melton was already standing. For a big, soft man, he looked implacably solid. "Blackmail is even more incredible than murder, for Alec. If you don't believe me, ask Lucy."

The inspector would as soon have put his head into a hungry lioness's mouth as to ask Lucy. "Blackmail is probably too strong a word. But something, or someone, was worrying Davin Lowry after the meeting yesterday. He wanted to come see Lucy last night and get her advice. Miss Dilworth had announced their engagement, and Lucy thought Lowry wasn't too sure he wanted to get married. Would you have any idea why?"

Melton shrugged and made a face, but it seemed a curiously hammed-up gesture. "Why ask me? Marriage is not quite my thing."

When McDougal got into his car and turned on the ignition, he fumed because the thing wouldn't start, till he found he had the indicator on Drive instead of Park. *I'm too old to go a night without sleep.* His mind kept on groping through a fog of weariness, and he thought he knew the next turn, but the way there was full of animate objects that might trip him up. Of these, his landlady was the most animate.

He found Lucy on her terrace, with her size-four feet tilted up on a chaise and a sketch pad in her lap. For some mystifying reason, the flagstones around the chaise were littered with birdseed. "I thought it would make me feel less sodden if I did birds today. But the stupid things won't come near. I got a cardinal on the apple tree, but the sketch didn't come off. I'm all thumbs."

He caught a swift glimpse of the top sketch on her pad—and it didn't look like a bird; it looked like a two-legged man—before she slapped the pad shut.

"Have you let Mario out of solitary?" She sounded cross and worried, and one lock of short curly hair stood straight up, always a sign of hectic thinking.

The inspector, already wary of coming right out with the main question on his mind, backed off and seized on Mario as the milder of two evils. He riffled mentally through the reasons he might advance for holding Mario. Drunk and disorderly . . . assaulted a police officer . . . refused to explain why his footprints show up over the victim's. . . . They all seemed too feeble for Lucy's saber-toothed rebuttal. So he said, "Mario refused to see a lawyer, and he insists on staying in jail. But Angie is on her way to see him now. I asked Terrizi to take her in to talk to Mario, to see if she could get some straight answers."

"Meaning you couldn't."

He grabbed for a new topic: "I just came from seeing Foster's friend Melton. Foster won't be back from the airport till noon or later, and I was trying to find out in the meantime why Foster seemed hostile to Lowry from the minute they met."

He saw Lucy glance swiftly at the sketch pad in her lap, before she tossed it onto the lower tier of the table beside her. "What did Bert say? I hope you didn't try to bully him."

To forestall her guessing that he'd bungled in handling her friend, he tried diversionary shock tactics. "Did you know Foster's youngest sister committed suicide by jumping out a window?"

"Oh, how horrible. Everything's horrible—starting last night. First Davin, and now Alec's sister. I think you should get us a drink. It's only eleven thirty, but it seems like pitch-black night. At least get yourself a beer. Even Scotland Yard drinks beer on duty. I'll have a sherry, but not just a thimbleful. I want a good slug in an old-fashioned glass."

McDougal brought the drinks and let her take a healthy gulp before he said, "Do you think the two deaths might have been connected?"

"What two deaths?" Her voice shrilled up. "Do you mean somebody else has been killed?"

"I meant Alec Foster's sister."

"But that must have been at least three years ago, before Alec and Bert came east. I'm sure that's what Alec meant about the aftershocks being worse than the earthquake. So how could that have anything to do with Davin Lowry?"

He told her why. "If, for instance, Foster recognized Lowry as the man who'd got his sister into trouble."

Lucy looked almost cheerful. "What a quaint phrase. I assume you mean pregnant. And no girl in her right mind would commit suicide just because she was pregnant. She'd have an abortion. Or if she were a celebrity she'd announce it to all the papers and have a contest for readers to guess the father."

"I doubt if she was pregnant." It didn't fit in with his theory. "Melton said she was on LSD. Lowry might have given her drugs."

"No." She sounded very sure, but then, Lucy was always sure. "Davin struck me as the fastidious, physical-fitness sort."

The inspector took another sip of ice-cold Löwenbräu Munich. "It was just a wild guess on my part."

She looked at him shrewdly, and her small, straight nose wrinkled as if she'd smelled a rat. "That's the first time I ever heard you admit a guess of yours was wild. You're softening me up for something. What are you leading up to, with all this skulking around Robin Hood's barn?"

"Well, I began thinking of the way you described Lowry. And I wondered if by any chance he might have been a homosexual."

He expected her to explode, but she sat very still and said in a small voice, "What put that into your head?"

McDougal marveled at how easy it was. "For one thing, you mentioned that Lowry picked out clothes for Grace Dilworth."

The explosion came then. "Of all the God-damn stupid reasons I ever heard! Hal often went shopping with me and helped me pick out new clothes. That's exactly the sort of thing you'd consider effeminate, you—you—" She couldn't think of an epithet nasty enough and ended in a splutter. "*You* probably never even noticed what your wife had on."

Most of the time, he hadn't. But now he remembered with hurting clarity: Eileen in a long red velveteen dress one Christmas eve, trimming their tree. . . . And a morning when he'd waked to see her standing by a bedroom window. She was wearing a sheer green nightgown, and as she opened the blinds, the sun had blazed in, outlining her figure dazzlingly. His whole body had come full awake, wanting her. Must have been a Sunday morning. Eileen had never been up on weekdays till long after he went to work. . . .

Lucy was still spluttering. ". . . and men who never notice what I wear strike me as stiff-legged clods."

McDougal said, "Get off your war horse. I need your help badly."

It was the magic password, for Lucy. "All right, but don't be such a damn self-righteous Philistine. You remind me of that old saying: 'Everybody's queer but me and thee, and even thee is a little queer!'"

"I only meant that you know homosexuals better than I do, as friends, and you're so much more aware of people. So I wanted to get your instinctive first impression of Lowry."

She was thoughtful, considering. "He was one of the handsomest men I'd ever seen. Not the pretty-boy type. Vitality and intelligence—and what I'm damned if I'll call 'charisma.' Sex appeal is good enough. When I meet a real male, he gives off a kind of crackle."

McDougal couldn't help wondering if he himself crackled.

She said matter-of-factly, "For example, I felt it when I first met you at the butcher's."

This was so gratifying the inspector said magnanimously, "Of course, we all have male and female traits in us."

"I should hope so. Otherwise men would be hopeless. Living in pigsties, grunting."

He suppressed a retort on lady pigs. "But your first impression of Lowry was that he was strongly male?"

"I'd say so. Of course, there's no test for it, like litmus paper. Somebody told me that in World War Two, the test at a New York induction center was to have a draftee twirl around on his toes. I guess if he was graceful, he was suspect."

Stop bilking the question, McDougal said silently.

"And there's no question in my mind that Davin was crazy about Grace."

"Then why was he reluctant to marry?"

"You're a great one to ask that. If I try to introduce you to a girl, you won't come nearer than fifty paces."

Women tossed illogical answers like bombs and waited for the thing to go off. McDougal said, with forbearance, "My case is a bit different. I'd already been married."

"But not till you were well into your thirties. Davin was younger. And some men are late starters." She was still hedging.

"You told me Alec Foster and Lowry bristled at each other from the start. Homosexuals are often that way."

Again she glanced involuntarily toward the sketch pad.

"I'd like to see your bird."

"What bird?" Lucy said absently. "Oh, that. No, I can't decide yet if it's worth showing."

The remark was suspiciously out of character.

"I wish Grace would wake up." Non sequiturs were definitely in character, but the inspector had a hunch this was no non sequitur, with Lucy: she wanted to find out something from Grace. "I made a fresh pot of coffee for her."

"I could do with some coffee myself," McDougal said cunningly. "This beer's made me even sleepier." Get her out of the way for five minutes.

Lucy dug her heels in. "It's on the stove. Help yourself."

Stalemate. The inspector made a show of consulting his watch with a grimace depicting, It's later than I thought. "I'd better get down to headquarters and see how Angie's making out with Sandini."

It was another sign of Lucy's preoccupation that she didn't heckle him again about letting Mario loose. And she hadn't asked about Myra Farmington's alibi either. After pushing Myra as the vindictive-killer mentality at breakfast, Lucy seemed to have dropped that notion like a cold potato.

On the way into Wingate, McDougal decided that he'd go back to his studio between twelve thirty and one. Grace ought to be up by then; Lucy would be fixing a tray for her guest, and McDougal could get his hands on the sketch pad.

He had no conscious plan to get his hands on Grace. Interview her, of course, as considerately as possible. She'd help him all she could. Extraordinarily well-balanced woman. And she shouldn't be alone in that monstrously big house right now. Lucy was right about that.

Sergeant Terrizi's girl Angie had almost never in her life had a waking moment alone, except perhaps in the bathroom. Seen anywhere, she would have been noticeable. But seen against the background of the grimy old police headquarters, in the basement of Town Hall, she was sensational. It wasn't just that she was pretty, and that her pink sheath was short enough to give her long, lissome legs full play, and that she moved like quicksilver; and it wasn't just that her black hair floated silkily about her shoulders or that her dark eyes were enormous, with improbably long, not glued-on, lashes. The more important thing was that Angela Vella had a quality that pulled men to her the way a windmill draws water. The fact that she wasn't shaped like a windmill helped, of course.

Chief Salter himself escorted her into his little office to wait while Sergeant Terrizi fetched Mario. The chief was an overworked, overweight man in his fifties who had once had an ulcer and still wore that pained expression. He was feeling on the defensive now: any favorite uncle of Angie's was the last man he wanted locked up, but his visitor said in her soft, sweet voice that she knew it was terribly hard on him when he already had so many problems. Somehow he found himself telling her in detail about a current headache: "We only got three cells, and no facilities for women. So what happens? More women turning to crime around here than ever before. Last week we caught two burglars in one night—both dames. Regular wildcats, they were. And no place to stow them. So with four men on night duty, two men have to take the women clear over to Bridgeport to jail, and that leaves one man on the desk and one to patrol the whole town. Good thing we didn't have to arrest any women last night, when this guy of Grace Dilworth's is found dead. As it was, we had to bring in every man off duty—Terrizi, Waters, Bayles, half a dozen others—and we still had to yell for help to Hartford. Troopers, more lab men, more detectives. They come in to write out their reports today and they're packed into the squad room like sardines in rancid oil."

Angie was liquidly sympathetic. "I do hope the inspector can find the real murderer soon." (The fact that they might already have the murderer locked up, in the disheveled person of Mario, was obviously too silly to even consider.) And once that's all solved, then the town ought to vote you the money to build a big, modern police headquarters, with room for women too." Her pretty lips curved up deliciously. "You ought to get Women's Lib on it."

Chief Salter said gallantly he'd rather get Angie on it. "If you'd present our case to the selectmen, they'd get the money for building even if they had to sell apples." The phone on his desk jangled. "Yes, she's to see him in here. I'll clear out so they can talk alone."

Three minutes later Mario was saying, "Angie baby, don't come too near me. I think I already picked up fleas here." He scratched unconvincingly. The truth was that the cells were much cleaner and tidier than the rest of the place, which occupied a total space of 1,235 square feet and featured peeling, grayish-green paint, fly-specked WANTED posters, bulging cardboard boxes used as extra file cabinets, and wastebaskets overflowing with soggy coffee containers and cigarette butts.

Angie didn't believe in the fleas, but she made oh-you-poor-darling noises. "Mama says you have to let her get a lawyer and get you out of here."

"That means bail," Mario said. "And I won't pay a cent of bail money because the cops get it."

"Uncle Mario, you know that's not true."

"Then who gets the bail money? The prisoner doesn't get it. Nobody's offering *me* twenty thousand dollars."

"I think they keep it in escrow or something."

"And then when I'm found innocent they give me half?" He spat on Chief Salter's linoleum.

"All we have to do is prove you're innocent, and then none of us will care what happens to the money. If you tell me exactly what happened—then poof, you're free."

This was a slightly oversimplified statement of police procedure, but coming from so pretty a girl, it was persuasive.

"Angie, I swear to you on the Virgin Mary I did not kill that son of a bitch. And whoever did, I'd shake their hand, but I don't know yet who to shake hands with." He'd refused to sit down; he was prowling around the small, crowded room with that tilting-forward Marx Brothers gait. As he went by a drab green file cabinet, he slapped it resoundingly.

"I believe you, darling. You know that. But if you'll just fill me in. . . . You went back to the rose garden after the concert. They found your footprints. Why did you go back there after you left the liquor store?"

"I'm driving by and I see somebody's turned on the sprinkler down there. Crazy thing to do, right after a rain. During the drought they were always yelling at me I use too much water— and then they turn around and run the sprinkler after a rain. So I went in through the back lot and turned it off there at the nozzle first."

"And then what?"

Mario stopped prowling. He stood in frozen silence which thawed into a dramatic shudder. "I went over to the steps and I think I'm having the d.t.'s. Me, a respectable, clean-drinking man—I'm seeing—well, like a hatrack made of swords and a man hanging on it."

"How awful for you." Her eyes were shining with tears. "What did you do then?" She was afraid she already knew.

"I scrammed," he said simply. "I went off and got drunk again so's I could sleep off the d.t.'s."

"Why didn't you tell Nicky right away?"

"Tell a cop I think I'm having d.t.'s?"

"But Nicky would have believed you had nothing to do with a killing. I mean he *knows* you didn't."

"So that's why he brought me to jail. You'd marry a cop who jailed your old uncle for turning off a sprinkler at the nozzle?"

"I'll tell Nicky that's all you did, and he'll be so relieved and happy."

103

Sergeant Terrizi wasn't all that happy over the story they had to tell the inspector.

"Would you like me to tell him for you?" Angie asked. "You'd tell it much more clearly, but maybe he'd like it firsthand. I mean, as long as I was the one who talked to Uncle Mario. . . ."

Sergeant Terrizi agreed that firsthand would be better. It wasn't a story that could be told clearly, but if anyone could make the thing sound better, it was Angie.

The inspector was in the squad room going over some lab findings on how footprints matched up with the casts. At the next table, Sergeant Bayles was interviewing a snaggle-toothed teenage boy who'd been caught shoplifting. In his lilting Jamaican voice Bayles was saying, "But what would you want with five pencil sharpeners, kid?"

"I didn't want the fuckin' things. I'm just doin' it to bug the pigs."

An exhausted-looking detective who had sat down at the other end of the table was munching a soggy egg sandwich. One low retching sound came out of him at the mention of pigs.

"Has your family got a TV?" Bayles asked.

The boy bared his fangs. "Yeah, and it was bought and paid for. So keep your dirty nigger hands off it."

Bayles didn't even blink; he just looked tireder. "Let's say one of your pals steals it 'to bug the pigs.' How would you like it?"

"I'd stick a knife in his guts."

"And the store owner who had the pencil sharpeners you stole —should he stick a knife in your guts?"

The detective stopped munching long enough to make a surreptitious "Right on" circle with the thumb and first finger of his free hand. He was small and roly-poly, with such dark circles under his eyes that somehow he looked like a raccoon. McDougal glanced over and recognized him. "Glad Hanson sent you down to help us out again." (Inspector Hanson had succeeded McDougal in Hartford two years before as head of the Connecticut State Police, when McDougal insisted on retiring early.) What the hell was this detective's name? Not Raccoon. He'd ask Hanson the next time they talked on the phone. But then he remembered. Carlin—that was it—Carlin.

"Real nasty murder you got," the detective said, as if congratulating the inspector on snagging such a gem.

McDougal said it certainly was.

"That little lady last summer—the one who told me where the murderer would have stashed the victim's handbag—Mrs. Ramsgate, wasn't it?—is she in on this one too?"

The inspector admitted Lucy Ramsdale had a certain tenuous connection with the case.

"Good," Raccoon-eyes said with enthusiasm. "Remember me to her, will you?"

As Bayles passed them with the shoplifter, McDougal said on impulse, "Sergeant, I'd be grateful if you could spare me a few minutes later, after you finish with this"—he glanced at the boy coolly—"small-time thief. I need your opinion on something."

"Yes, Inspector." Bayles was looking less tired as he strode off after the boy.

Raccoon-eyes, who was facing the door into the hall, said "*Wow!* Look what Terrizi's got hold of! If she's another shoplifter, I'd give her the store."

McDougal reacted on a split track. The sight of Angie advancing radiantly made him glad he had more male than female traits. And the sight of Terrizi made him think of something he actually did want Bayles's help on. Something that might be important. A third track of thought, that Angie wouldn't look so delighted if she hadn't got something positive out of Mario Sandini, made his welcome even warmer.

"Inspector, it's wonderful to see you again." Angie took his long, lean hand in both of her own. "Thank goodness you're on this case."

The inspector was suddenly thankful himself. All things seemed possible, even a quick solution. "Sit down with me and tell me what you found out."

Raccoon-eyes, after a bewildered moment for readjustment, said *sotto voce* to Terrizi, "She the dead man's fiancey? She shouldn't have any trouble finding replacements."

"She's my girl friend." So might a man have said, simply, "I have the Kohinoor diamond in my pocket."

But just as the possession of the Kohinoor diamond raises certain apprehensions in the owner, the sergeant was having nervous side effects. Was Angie being too breezy? Could she really tell Mario's story so that it sounded good?

She and the inspector were in earnest conversation at the other end of the table. Like most good conversations, one was talking and the other listening with flattering attention and asking intelligent questions.

After several minutes of this, Terrizi heard Angie say, loud and clear, "And I know Uncle Mario was telling the truth because I can always tell when he's lying."

The inspector glanced over and smiled broadly. "Remember that, sergeant, after you're married."

The sergeant next thought his ears must be going soft. Could the inspector actually be calling Angie "my dear"? He was. "My dear, you got just the information we needed. Somebody deliberately turned on the sprinkler, either to get Mario back into the garden, or to make the ground around there even muddier and make it harder for us to identify footprints. Mario did us a big favor by turning off the sprinkler fast. And we've already found his prints coming in through the back lot, so that checks out."

"So may I take Uncle Mario home with me right now?"

This was just a wee bit rushing the fences. The inspector said there were one or two more points he wanted to check with her uncle. "But if Chief Salter agrees, I'm sure we can release him by this afternoon."

In an excess of emotion, Angie blew a kiss to McDougal as she left. Two kisses, in fact.

Sergeant Terrizi was afraid this might be carrying girlish informality too far, but the inspector didn't look as if he minded. He didn't blow kisses back, but he had the air of a man who considers it. And when Terrizi came back after seeing Angie to her car, a duty which somehow took eleven minutes for a walk of a hundred yards, the inspector was still genial. He didn't seem to have noticed the time lapse.

"I took a call from the West Coast in Salter's office," he said. "The detective who handled the case when Foster's young sister committed suicide. It's true she was on an LSD trip, but she'd gone onto drugs because she'd married a man who turned out to be a homo, a closet fag. She came home one day and found him in bed with his lover. After the suicide, Foster went wild, swore he'd kill the husband if he ever laid hands on him. The husband skipped off to Mexico with his homo friend, and they're checking on him now. His name wasn't Lowry, but they don't know the name of the lover. Melton got Foster calmed down, and it was Melton who set things up so they could move to the East. I got a report from the lab, and Foster's footprints are definitely grouped with Lowry's in the garden and again near the top of the steps. If Foster got home soon after eleven—and I'm inclined to think Melton is honest about that—then he wouldn't have had time to do the killing and soap the steps and—" McDougal stopped dead and looked startled. "The steps were soaped *afterward* to make them seem more slippery. So it would be passed off as accidental death. Not cause—just effect."

It was pleasant to have the young sergeant looking at him again with total admiration. They discussed this new theory, and everything seemed to fit. "And your idea of somebody using a bicycle . . . I think Foster drove home so that Melton would think he was safely settled in for the night. Then he must have gone back by bicycle—Melton says he'd have heard the car—to take care of setting the scene afterward. Find out if Foster has a bicycle. And I'll get Sergeant Bayles to take a little bike trip and see how much time it might take from Foster's to the Center and back. Bayles is a Jamaican, so that probably means he's an expert cyclist, but he ought to be able to gauge how long it would take a nonexpert to do three miles each way."

The sergeant's eyes, normally the size of jumbo shiny black olives, squinted in worriment. "It would have only taken Foster ten or so minutes to soap the steps and turn on the sprinkler or whatever. So why wouldn't he stay there and do all that at one time, instead of driving home and then taking that long bicycle ride back?"

"Maybe he didn't think of the soap trick till after he was home. And even if he'd thought of it early, he couldn't risk being seen soaping the steps so soon after the concert. He had to wait till after midnight, when the town's fairly dead."

The somnolence of Wingate night life was a grievance of Terrizi's. Even the Purple Pizza Palace closed early. From pizza, his thoughts went to Angie as naturally as a crow flies backward or forward.

Bayles came back to the squad room and his face lit up as the inspector described the new assignment. "Allow for traffic being much lighter at night. And if there's a back road even part way, use it. I think the person we're checking on would have avoided the main highway as much as possible." McDougal went into details on what he wanted.

Bayles said, "Even if I'm not in uniform, a lot of people know me around here, and they might wonder how come I'm biking on a weekday. Wouldn't it look more natural if Zora went with me on her bike? I mean—more like a pleasure jaunt?"

Terrizi, having seen Zora and feeling refortified in his own love life, generously supported his colleague's suggestion.

"If Miss Dilworth is staying on at Mrs. Ramsdale's," Bayles went on, "Zora could get off any time. By the way, she said to tell you she's remembered the name of the friend Miss Dilworth gave her father's bicycle to—it was Mr. Foster."

The inspector looked smug. The wind was blowing the way he wanted it. "Ask Chief Salter if he can spare you right now. I'd like you to go as soon as possible."

Terrizi began to worry whether he himself would be dragooned to take over the desk while Bayles went off. "The chief was telling Angie we're twice as shorthanded now that more women are taking to crime."

The inspector, who was making notes in a small, black leather memo book, said "Mmmm" absently.

The sergeant had hoped McDougal would take the hint and let him interview suspects or something so he wouldn't be hauled back to mundane chores. He said more loudly, "It's almost twelve thirty. Shouldn't Miss Dilworth be awake now?"

Coming on top of his chattiness about more women taking to crime, the effect of the question was unfortunate.

"Are you still harping on that business of shooting the heads off marigolds? Forget it. I'll take care of seeing Miss Dilworth." The inspector was no longer genial.

10

Lucy had got out the drawing pad again and was staring at the quick sketch she'd done two hours before: Davin Lowry reconstructed from memory. Or not so much reconstructed as lifted like a photographic slide from the file in her painter's memory. But it wasn't Davin as she'd seen him, a strongly handsome, smiling man coming up the path at the Center arm in arm with Grace. That was what she'd meant to sketch, to reassure herself. Instead, it was another Davin she'd pulled out of her mind: Davin as he'd been after Alec and the board members had reacted badly to his plans for the sculpture garden. This Davin looked petulant, almost pouty, as if he were about to toss his head and stamp his foot. But petulance was as much a male trait as female, Lucy thought. More. She'd known more petulant men than women. Having settled that point, she glanced at the sketch more cheerfully, then frowned again. The head with that faun's peak—surely the peak hadn't been that pronounced in real life. So Peter Pannish, somehow. But it wasn't Peter Pan's *head* that had been pointed; it was his hat. Of course, how silly.

I'm superimposing all that talk about homosexuals on the man I actually saw. I'm distorting everything, and it's all McDougal's fault. Imagine his thinking that it was effeminate of Davin to help Grace pick out clothes. Hal would have roared.

She remembered the time in Paris when Hal had gone with her to a Marcel Rochas boutique. They'd picked out a blouse and hat, and she'd worn them to lunch at—what was the name of that restaurant—something Lilacs? A Frenchman lunching with another man at a table near the Ramsdales kept staring at her, and Hal finally had got cross about it. They'd quarreled when they got back to their little hotel on the Left Bank. Hal said she'd deliberately encouraged the man to stare. And Lucy said, "I did not. I can't help the way I look."

But she *had* encouraged the man. A woman can turn herself off so that a man, even across a room, knows she's not interested. Or she can keep sending out rays just for fun, to keep her hand in. And it had been such an enchanting hat, like a bonnet in that Renoir painting of the girl sitting in a wicker chair at the seaside. But no white ruching, just a deliciously wicked little veil, and one pink flower under the brim. I tried it on again for Hal after I was undressed that night. And he came over to kiss me . . . and then later he said, "It's better with your hat off." I never made love in a hat. I should have, sometime.

She remembered their lying in bed afterward, in their hotel room on a courtyard. It had been August, and a non-air-conditioned August, with everybody's windows open. Two women in the room above theirs had quarreled noisily, yelling accusations at each other. One had been unfaithful, or the other one thought she had. Hal had said, "Lovers' quarrels always sound worse when they're both one sex."

If Alec and Davin had been lovers once on the West Coast, if they'd arranged to meet secretly at the Center and then quarreled. . . . But Alec and Bert Melton had such a good relationship. They were genuinely happy together. Alec wouldn't want anybody else. And anyway, Davin was engaged to Alec's boss; he had been unmistakably crazy about Grace. But had he really crackled, as she'd told McDougal? Sparks jumping? Or was it more the bright glow of an electric grate? She looked uneasily at the sketch. Sound out Grace in some devious way, before saying anything to the inspector. Twelve forty-five; why didn't that girl wake up? Had the police doctor given her too strong a dosage? Grace was in the guest room over the kitchen, and Lucy debated whether to go out and bang pans around, or hold up an iron skillet and drop it. The biggest omelet pan would make a rousing crash. Maybe instead of breakfast, Grace would be ready for a real meal, maybe ginger pancakes with crab meat, to tempt her appetite. It was tempting Lucy's appetite so strenuously she went right out and made herself a test batch of pancakes.

A good thing she had her lunch without waiting for her guest. Grace appeared on the terrace just before one and refused anything but black coffee. "I'm still too groggy to eat. I've never taken a sleeping pill before—not even when Sam died—and the injection knocked me out so completely I don't even remember saying good night to you."

She was in the same dark slacks, pullover and sneakers she'd worn the night before, and Lucy thought, How could she bear ever to put them on again? Not that the clothes were blood-stained, but they no longer seemed like clothes on a living woman. Grace's blank, staring eyes reminded Lucy of somebody in hypnosis. She poured more coffee for her guest and made a determined effort to talk normally. "Zora brought over other clothes for you, and I put them in my room. I was going to tell you as soon as I heard you stirring, but I didn't hear a sound."

Grace said in a faraway voice, "Sam used to say you had ears like a fox."

"A deer would be a more flattering comparison," Lucy complained. "The shy, beautiful wild thing, bounding away at the faintest sound." But she was rather hurt by the phrase: like a fox indeed! As if she were crafty or something. Her ego reacted bouncily; high time she got some credit: "It's a damn good thing I *did* hear you go into my garage last night. When I think that you might have gone driving off to the Center alone. . . ."

Grace murmured that the inspector had been so good to her. "After we found—" she bit her lip, controlling herself rigidly.

"McDougal told me how extraordinarily brave you were. But, Grace dear, don't try to be too stoic and self-contained about this. And don't stay in that big house alone just yet. Stay with me. I'm being selfish in asking that, because I'd worry constantly about you."

"When I woke up, I wished I were dead."

"Of course you did. That's only human. I wished it over and over after Hal died. He'd been the mainspring of my life for almost forty years, and I felt like a stopped clock that's no good to anybody. But you're still young, and Davin told me that seeing you change, seeing you come fully alive—a whole, lovely woman—and knowing he'd helped, was the most wonderful feeling he'd ever had."

Grace's eyes were no longer blank. They were sad, haunted, but the glaze of shock had lifted. "Did he really say that?"

"He said much more. He told me he cared more about you than he'd ever cared about anybody in his life."

Tears spilled over, then. Grace seemed not even to know she was weeping, as if the tear ducts were divorced from the rest of her. "You won't believe this, but I was still a virgin when I met him, and I'm almost thirty-three."

You're almost thirty-nine, Lucy corrected silently. But she considered that lying about one's age was a healthy sign in a woman.

"He was so exactly right for me, in every way."

Unmistakably Grace meant, Right in bed too.

"But he was worried about the idea of marrying somebody with so much money. That's what he wanted to talk to you about when he asked to come over and see you last night."

So that was it. Lucy felt on the verge of weeping herself. "I'll blame myself forever that I didn't let him come."

"Imagine how much more awful I feel. I could have done something when he first suggested taking out those stairs down to the garden. He wanted to put in a ramp, and I said there was plenty of time to think about it. But then the stairs killed him. That's the hardest thing for me to face."

Lucy hesitated. It seemed inhuman to let Grace blame herself, thinking it had been a senseless accident on the stairs. If the inspector was right, it was murder, and even at Lucy's most biased she was of the grudging opinion that Mac knew what he was talking about, at least on murder. She had also read enough detective stories to know that the police like to break such news themselves. In books, they always got a clump of suspects into one room and announced, "It wasn't an accident—it was mur-

113

der," then looked in ten directions at once, to watch everybody's first reaction and spot the guilty one. Guilt standing out like a scarlet A on the chest. The police would never spot *me*, Lucy thought, with complacence.

But she was jolted back to concern by Grace's anguish. To hell with waiting for the inspector to break the news. "I won't have you blaming yourself this way—" she began, when the phone rang. The screen door opening off the terrace stuck, and as she yanked at it furiously, she thought, Damn Mac, I thought he said he'd planed the bottom edge. She was cross and out of breath by the time she'd half run across the long living room to get to the phone.

When she came back, she was smiling. "Dear, your maid wants to speak to you. And I told her I insist on your staying here a few nights at least, so you just tell her what you want done."

Grace was gone several minutes, and when she came back she looked better. More alert. She sounded almost like herself. "I told Zora there was no point in her staying there any longer today. She said Fred Thorndike had called several times, but she just said I was asleep and didn't tell him where I was because she was afraid he'd call here and wake me. And of course the Farmingtons left messages." She made a face that expressed what she thought of the Farmingtons. "But it's odd Alec didn't call. We've been so close."

Lucy thought this was a slight exaggeration, but understandable. In that hypersensitive, quivering state of the newly bereaved, there's a feeling that the world should revolve around one's own tragedy; any friend who didn't respond instantly and drop everything else, was callous, cold, cruel. Lucy explained about Alec's having to take the concert pianist to the airport. "Anyway, when he left he didn't know it was—" She caught herself just in time. No point in telling Grace now. "He didn't know how long you'd sleep."

"If I could just sleep forever," Grace said. "No, I mustn't talk that way. Sam wouldn't like it."

"Neither would Davin. He was so proud of the way you'd come out of your—well, your cocoon."

"He brought me out of it," Grace said softly. "On the ship we played deck tennis in a doubles match and won. But when he asked me to have a drink afterward, I was so nervous I couldn't think of anything to say. I just wanted to sit and look at him. Every woman on the ship was eying him—he was the most attractive man on board. The first few times we walked on deck together, I kept thinking some prettier, younger girl would latch onto him and take him away. You know, Lucy, I lied to you. I'm really almost thirty-nine."

Try to keep that a secret around Wingate, Lucy thought. Aloud, she said, "Davin told me you made every other woman look fluffy."

The tears started again, but in a quieter way. Grace dabbed at her eyes with a paper napkin. "When I was with him, I somehow took on his sureness. It was as if his being so handsome and charming were a magic cloak he threw over me so that it covered both of us. Soon I felt *we* were the most attractive couple." Her hand closed convulsively on the napkin. "Now nothing's left. I don't even have a snapshot of him. I tried to take pictures of him whenever we went on shore, but he said he couldn't stand those home-movie effects of 'This is Ed in front of Michelangelo's whatsit.' He had me photograph beautiful pieces by themselves, and I knew it was because he really cared about art—he didn't want to superimpose his own image on some piece he thought was important. But if I just had one picture of him, it would comfort me."

All Lucy's most loving, generous instincts surged up. "I did a rough sketch from memory, if you'd like to have that. But it's not very good."

Grace leaned over and grabbed Lucy's hand. "Oh, anything! Besides, you couldn't do a bad sketch."

Lucy agreed. She produced the pad and handed it over.

Grace flipped the sheets eagerly, barely glancing at several earlier sketches Lucy considered worth commenting on. She tried to make allowances, although when tribute was due she was accustomed to exacting full measure.

Her guest had come to the sketch of Davin now, and was

studying it. "He looks cross," she said softly. "The way he looked when Alec was so unpleasant at the meeting. He resented Davin so terribly. Davin tried to reassure him—they even went to his office after the meeting to talk, but Alec was still so bitter, and so against the sculpture garden. And that upset Davin. You caught that feeling in your sketch. You have such an uncanny way of sensing people's moods."

All very flattering, but Lucy couldn't enjoy it properly because she was worried at the direction the conversation had taken. If the inspector heard Grace talking that way about Alec, it could be dangerous.

She said quickly, "Fred Thorndike was even more bitter."

"Poor old Fred. One reason he was so furious about Davin was that it was Fred who urged me to go on that cruise. I'll always bless him for that. But I won't let him have a hand in doing the sculpture garden. I'm going to do it exactly the way Davin planned, as a memorial."

Oh, brother, there goes our parking lot. But Grace needs a project to steady her. And Alec and I might be able to talk her out of some of the wildest pieces.

"I think I'll go home for a while and get the plans." Grace actually had some color in her face now. Lucy was doubly relieved because she'd been hesitant about leaving Grace alone while she did her afternoon's stint at the Thrift Shop.

"Zora said some detective found the color slides of the sculpture in the guest room and took them away, but he wouldn't have taken the plans and our notes. Would you like to see them?"

"I'd love it." If Grace persists in this, she may get herself killed like Davin. But of course she doesn't know yet he *was* killed. Well, I'm not going to give her another shock now, when she's just beginning to revive. I'll let Mac tell her tonight. "I'll expect you for dinner. And the inspector will be here."

Grace brushed her hand across her cheek in the old nervous habit. "Is—is Inspector McDougal interested in art too?"

"Oh, yes." That would certainly be news to the inspector. "He has an unusual sense of design." Especially if it's a diagram of a dead body. "He'd be fascinated."

Good thing she'd made the beef bourguignon and got the anchovy-and-onion filling ready for the tarts this morning. Wouldn't be time to market after she left the Thrift Shop at five. Pick up some more wine. Do Grace good to have a mildly alcoholic evening. If only Mac doesn't upset her. Better get that part over with early.

"If you come back by five thirty, then the inspector will have time to talk to you alone while I'm in the kitchen." And he won't talk about art.

Grace understood. "It was so good of him not to bother me with questions earlier. By tonight I'll be able to talk about the accident. One of the things I have to do this afternoon that I dread is to make the—the arrangements for—" She broke off, shivering.

Lucy didn't offer to help, on that. She thought funerals were barbaric, and if Grace wanted the kind of overdone, masochistic spectacular Sam's funeral had been, then she wanted no part in it.

"I think I'll get hold of Fred and ask him to see the undertaker."

Get your ex-suitor to bury your lover. It sounded rather ghoulish. But Fred might even enjoy it.

"For me, Davin will never be dead." Grace was looking at the sketch again, brooding. Then she removed it from the pad, very carefully, along the perforation. "I want to take it home for now because I have a silver frame I think will fit it perfectly. You don't know what you've done for me."

Lucy, warmed by her own thoughtfulness, watched Grace stride over to the stone wall between the two properties. Grace was holding the sketch against her chest, blank side out, so that nothing could brush against her treasured new possession.

If Mac wants to see it later, he can ask Grace. But it might have given him the wrong impression at the start, and he's so prejudiced he'd pick on Alec at the slightest pretext. Lucy did an eeny, meeny, miney, mo in her mind, on other possible suspects. If she had to throw somebody to the wolves, it should be somebody she didn't care about. Had the old-time czarists really thrown serfs off the back of a sleigh, one at a time, to appease pursuing wolves? As this image crunched in her mind, she felt rather queasy. Why couldn't Davin's death be an accident? Because of the soap. Flora Pollit was hipped on using laundry soap instead of foamy detergent, but Flora wouldn't go that far to demonstrate her point; it would give soap a bad name. Anyway, the killer had to be somebody who was thwarted, and Flora wasn't thwarted; she was sounding off in every antipollution huddle in Fairfield County, and she'd won the battle against spraying the trees for worms. And she'd been against the parking lot, so in a way she'd won on that too.

Martha Teague had been for the parking lot, but by nature she was a wholesome appeaser, wanting to keep everybody happy, which made her a bore but not lethal. The Farmingtons? George had the mentality of a banker, and bankers didn't commit murder. Not much. They had less messy ways of ruining somebody. Myra? Lucy had long since cooled on that notion. Unless truth was a damn sight stranger than mystery fiction, the writers of anonymous letters weren't apt to kill; murder was too huge a gamble for them. They dispensed evil in smaller, sneakier ways.

So that left only poor Fred. He did have the strongest motive: Davin hadn't just taken over Grace, he had taken over the landscaping of the grounds Fred had been so naïvely proud of. Lucy sat peacefully embroidering a case against Fred as a murderer. The constant bzzzzzzz of a bee circling near her right ear had a soporific monotony. She had had less than five hours' sleep the night before, and she drifted into a doze.

She woke with a start to see her newest candidate for killer bending over her.

Her first flash reaction was fear: My police-siren flashlight's upstairs. But this was superseded instantly by an indignant feeling that Fred looked even more ineffectual than usual; he'd *shrunk*. If he was going to be exposed as a killer, then the least he could do was live up to the part. Such a colorless, neat little man, with that toothbrush moustache that looked pasted on. But then Lucy noticed that his waistcoat—he always wore some sort of vest, even in summer—was buttoned gee-haw, with a gap halfway up. For Fred to miss buttoning himself up one by one, in consecutive order, was a screaming indication that something was wrong.

"I'm sorry if I startled you." His voice was neat and clipped as usual; only the misbuttoned vest betrayed agitation. "I wanted to see Grace as soon as she woke up. The maid finally told me she was here."

"She's already gone," Lucy said. Did Fred have a gun? No bulge detectable. And if he tried to attack Grace, Grace was big enough to push back and knock him down. "Why don't you sit down and relax? I'll get you a beer." And phone Mac from the kitchen.

Fred refused to be plied with malt. He was being tiresomely single-minded. "Where did Grace go?"

"To get her hair done," Lucy said hurriedly. The maid must already have left, and if Fred knew Grace was alone in that house, and then he learned she was going ahead with the sculpture garden. . . .

"To get her *hair* done! It seems a peculiar time to get her hair done."

"For—uh—the funeral."

"I thought the police were holding the body for an autopsy. And a detective named Walter or Water or something came by and asked me for a shoe. Why should the police want my shoe?"

"They got a shoe from everybody."

"Everybody in town? Next they'll be lining us up by the hundreds for fingerprints."

"They already have our fingerprints. Don't you remember? Two years ago. For identification in case of 'nuclear incident.'" She sniffed. "If you're pulverized by a nuclear bomb, I doubt if there's enough left to identify."

"I do hope Grace decides on cremation," Fred said fussily. "Under the circumstances."

"Grace is going to call you about that. She wanted you to take care of the funeral arrangements."

Fred, who was perched on the edge of a deck chair, looked as if he were going to keel over. "I can't do that. It wouldn't be right."

This showed a sense of fitness Lucy approved of. If you killed somebody, you didn't volunteer as chief mourner, or serve as an undertaker's mouthpiece. "Why don't you go home and wait for her call?"

"I have to see Alec first. He's been gone all morning, but I know he always comes home for lunch. It's almost two now, but he's not at the Center and Martha Teague says he often eats late. I have to talk to him before I—" He broke off and fingered the knot in his narrow string tie. "I do wish Grace hadn't gone to get her hair done. In a town this size, it might cause talk. They'd think she was unfeeling."

"It was my idea that she get her hair done," Lucy said truthfully, if ambiguously. "I thought it would buck her up. Like putting on fresh mascara so you won't muck it up crying."

"Does she seem very upset?"

"Terribly. She's going to go ahead with the sculpture garden as a memorial to him." Oh, God, I'm a large-mouth idiot.

Fred had leaped up and was flapping his arms like a rooster. "It's crazy. You'll have to persuade her to stop."

"We'll all try to talk her out of it," Lucy said soothingly. "Don't worry about it right now."

"I'm worried about everything." He seemed embarrassingly close to tears. "After I see Alec, may I come back this afternoon to talk to you privately? There's something I want to tell you."

That would keep him away from Grace. Get Janie Trask to take over at the Thrift Shop, but she'd have to rush to make the arrangements. She was due there at two thirty. "Of course you may, Fred." Get hold of McDougal before Fred came back. But I'd better let Fred talk to me alone first. If he wants to confess, he'll be more apt to do it that way. Poor demented little man, she thought with compassion. I'll visit him every month in prison, and send him books and things.

As soon as Fred had gone off in his spotless little sedan—he washed it every Saturday morning and had been seen to dab at a speck of dust with a Kleenex—Lucy called Alec to warn him, but gave up after ten empty rings. Janie Trask said she'd be glad to take over the stint at the Thrift Shop, but she'd have to leave at four forty-five because she had promised to take her daughter and four other Brownie Scouts on a hike and cookout. "I don't want to take them too far." Privately, Lucy thought even a hundred yards would be too far.

"Is there a stream in that woods behind you?" Janie asked. The woods were actually part of the Dilworth property; Lucy said there was a stream. There were also a lot of mean brambles, but she didn't say that because it would have sounded inhospitable, especially after Janie had done her a favor.

"What a tragedy for Grace Dilworth."

Lucy lowered her voice to a hush. "Yes, she's staying here. That's why I can't go to the Thrift Shop today."

This got her off the hook in time to call police headquarters. Sergeant Terrizi answered, sounding dispirited, and said the inspector was in with Chief Salter, and then he was coming to see Miss Dilworth. "He got held up by some long-distance calls. She's awake now, isn't she?"

Lucy explained Grace had gone home. "She needs a little more time to pull herself together, but he can interview her here at five thirty. And tell him he's to have dinner with us." Should she say Fred Thorndike would be coming earlier? No, Mac would dash over and be too constraining. Just keep her police-siren flashlight handy.

"Oh, here's the inspector now."

"I don't need to talk to him," Lucy said hastily. Much better not. And she didn't want him home just yet, not even to make himself a sandwich. "Nicky, make sure he gets something to eat there."

The sergeant transmitted Lucy's messages to McDougal, but he knew better than to say straight out, "She wants you to eat lunch now."

"There'll be more lab reports coming over any minute. If you want to go over them now, I could order you a sandwich. Ham on white O.K.?"

Ham on white was O.K. Terrizi ordered a sandwich for himself too. He had hoped to do better; he had offered to escort Mario home himself, figuring Angie's mother would be so grateful she'd ask him in to have lunch, to share in the feast she'd have fixed for the prodigal's return. But Mario had refused to cooperate in this plan; he still thought his niece's betrothed had deliberately put him in jail because he'd turned off a sprinkler at the nozzle. Or at least, that's what he claimed. So he'd gone off alone, with his old felt hat restored to the back of his head. Mario would have the feast. The sergeant would have tuna on rye.

The inspector took off the lid of the cardboard container, confidently expecting to find the iced coffee he'd asked for. He stared at the contents, appalled: some thick gooey liquid the color of pale mud. "What's this?"

"It's a chocolate milkshake with vanilla ice cream," Terrizi said. "I thought it would be more nourishing."

The inspector scowled. "You drink it. And get me iced coffee."

At two twenty, a trooper reported that Alec Foster was back in town.

By four thirty, Lucy was in a high-voltage rage because she'd been stood up; she had stayed away from the Thrift Shop to listen sympathetically to a murderer's confession, but Fred Thorndike hadn't turned up.

11

It was the most frustrating, nobody-here day the inspector could ever remember professionally. Fred Thorndike was still not at home. Alec Foster seemed to be nowhere. His housemate, Bert Melton, wasn't at the Way Back Antiques Shop; the owner of the shop reported Bert had gone home late to lunch and hadn't returned. "Which is so unlike him I thought he might have got sunstroke or something, working on that terrace of theirs. He doesn't answer his phone and I can't leave the shop to go see."

Even Alec's assistant, Martha Teague, wasn't in her cubicle of an office adjoining Alec's at the Center. And her footprints, like those of the other three missing suspects, had showed up in the rose garden.

At three forty, Inspector McDougal stood in Alec Foster's office, looking unreceptively at a poster above the neat blond-wood desk:

ALL KNOTTED UP?
UNWIND BY MAKING DECORATIVE KNOTS
IN OUR NEW COURSE IN MACRAMÉ
The ancient craft that's once more sweeping the country
$10 for 12 lessons
First lesson: Lutestring Choker or Scarab Belt

A companion poster listed other courses for those who weren't knotty-minded:

Candle Making
Oshibana
Early American Decoration
Weaving (two methods)
Needlepoint
China Painting
Pottery
Caning

A pleasant, plump woman McDougal had met in the lobby on the way in said she thought Martha Teague was teaching weaving that afternoon. "The kind you do without a loom—just your hands. But I'm not sure which classroom. I know where the regular weaving course is given—in the room with the looms—but if all she needs is her hands she might be *anywhere.*" The woman said that if Mr.—uh—McDougal cared to stop by, she'd be delighted to show him some of the "lovely crafts items" for sale in the Center's gift shop downstairs. She was working there that afternoon, as a volunteer.

McDougal had backed out of that one with a minimum of words, but seeing the volunteer reminded him that Lucy was doing her stint at the Thrift Shop this afternoon, safely surrounded by other women. With four possible suspects loose and peculiarly unavailable, it was just as well Lucy wasn't in a vulnerable spot, being cosy with a killer. He found himself wondering if she'd remembered to make the anchovy-and-onion tarts before she went off to the Thrift Shop. Her memory was apt to be scattery, but not on food. He thought of the tarts with a pleasurable stirring of the gastric juices.

Grace Dilworth would be there for dinner, and he thought of Grace with a stirring of something else. He liked her self-contained manner, her quiet dignity. Although *dignity* wasn't the right word: too stiff. She'd been touchingly human the night before, turning to walk away so he wouldn't see the agony almost tearing her apart. And she hadn't come apart. Whatever the effort, and it must have been enormous, she'd shown a quality of courage he'd seldom met up with in a woman. The inspector, who prided himself on almost never showing his feelings, saluted her in his mind.

As he left Alec Foster's office, he stopped to look at the portrait of Sam Dilworth. Or, rather, it stopped him, like an active, jutting-out presence. Looked like the kind of man who'd try to dominate a daughter and surround her, which might explain why Grace had gone overboard on Davin Lowry, because he was so different from Daddy. No matter what the Freudians said, Mc-Dougal didn't believe most girls sought out a father image to marry. They were more apt to grab onto the pendulum and ride in the opposite direction. His ex-wife certainly had. Eileen's father had been, by all accounts, a charming, witty, man-about-clubs sort, with the built-in assurance a solid gold pedigree gives. If Eileen hadn't inherited money of her own . . . if she'd been less independent financially . . . but Eileen would have been independent even if she hadn't had two cents of her own. For one thing, she'd always been a beauty, and that too was solid gold coin of the realm. Grace Dilworth, who wasn't a beauty, would be much more inclined than Eileen to be influenced by a husband. But not malleable, like Silly Putty. Grace had a solidity of her own, and yet she wasn't mannish.

Thinking appreciatively of all the ways Grace Dilworth hadn't been mannish, or looked mannish, the night before, the inspector wandered down a short flight of stairs in search of Martha Teague. He passed an open door and glanced in, and the plump volunteer he'd met in the lobby hailed him as a friend: "So you did come! I'm so glad. We just love to show off."

It would have been churlish after that to refuse to go in. The inspector was not above being churlish if he had a definite place to go, or if his nose was twitching on a scent, but this case had too many vague scents and too many absentees. So he let himself be led on a round of glass display cases: sea shells glued onto plaques with seaweed artfully draped in and out; tasseled woven shopping bags; hand-painted pink and blue bridge tallies; silver bracelets that looked as if they'd been pummeled with enthusiasm; wrought or overwrought iron lamp bases; a dozen ceramic salt and pepper shakers that looked like toadstools, in a poisonous yellow green; some large squares of quite handsome tweed, and another display of weaving with rows that lurched in a drunken zigzag. "This is Martha Teague's sample of the new loomless weaving. Isn't it interesting? So free-form."

The inspector could only manage a grunt. Besides, he considered three minutes enough time to waste.

"If you go right on down that corridor, you're bound to find Martha in one of those rooms."

The classroom next to the gift shop was small, and as the inspector looked in, his interest quickened and focused: a woman was lying on one of the long work tables, and several other women were fanning her vigorously with magazines. "Mrs. Teague?" he said, half expecting somebody to point to the prostrate form on the table. "What happened?"

It wasn't Mrs. Teague. It was a Mrs. Voorhies, who had been painting a tray with gold leaf and had been overcome by the fumes. "We'd shut the door after the instructor went out, and I guess we shouldn't have," one of the resuscitating ladies explained cheerfully. "Gold is such *tricky* stuff."

The inspector withdrew hurriedly, before he could be drawn into a discussion of the trickier aspects of gold, a subject which seemed to baffle even the international experts.

Nobody was in the large room next door, but when McDougal realized it was the Center's art gallery, he took a quick glance around anyway. He spotted two of Lucy's water colors, and a dozen of a decidedly different caliber, hung on the tan burlap-covered walls.

He remembered Lucy saying crossly, "Amateurs don't suddenly decide to be doctors or scientists or lawyers. So what the hell makes them think they can suddenly be painters?" The inspector had remarked casually it was like all the amateurs who thought they could be detectives.

The remark had not been well received.

Sergeant Terrizi had come in the back door of the Center and had started working his way down the same corridor from the opposite end, in search of either Alec or Martha Teague. Now he was standing in the doorway of a classroom, listening to the instructor of something called hairpin crochet. He couldn't get anybody's attention to ask if the middle-aged woman instructor was Martha Teague; they were listening too raptly. The sergeant was not at his keenest that afternoon, and he too listened, though foggily, waiting for the moment when he might decently interrupt.

"Ladies, you *must count your loops*. And after counting, use two pins crisscrossed to mark the spot. Remember, X marks the spot."

The eight or ten women in the audience giggled courteously. The one man in the group, a paunchy baldhead, simply looked worried. The sergeant was rather worried himself—to find a man mixed up in this hairpin crochet. Sissy kind of thing to do. One uncle of Terrizi's had taken up needlepoint, but the family had kept it hushed up. To come right out with it like this, in a passel of women, seemed blatant.

"For the gaucho slit skirt," the instructor was saying, "you will need three-ply Wintuk Sport yarn. Or if you'd prefer to start out by making your husband a tie, the motif tie is a great favorite with men. For instance, if he plays tennis or golf, a golf club or a racquet is the perfect motif. You'll find the basic pattern on page twenty of your instruction book. Let's turn to that. For Round One, work two single crochet and join in a ring with a slip stitch to top of Chain Two. If you have too many stitches, use a larger crochet hook. Now in Round Two. . . ."

The sergeant was rather intrigued with the idea of a motif tie. Angie knitted very nicely; she had already done him a cable-stitch sweater and socks. She could do a tie with one hand clenched behind her back. But what motif should he tell her? He didn't play golf or tennis, or go fishing or scuba diving. *Cop—gun*. He felt oddly upset to realize a gun was the most likely motif for a cop—maybe the only one. If people knew how seldom we use a gun, he brooded. *We* don't go around shooting the heads off marigolds. He was still exacerbated over the way the inspector had told him off again on the subject of Grace Dilworth.

It had happened when Terrizi, looking over the charts on footprints, had pointed out that Miss Dilworth's prints showed at the top of the stairs right beside Lowry's, and then again down in the rose garden in several places. "But she said they left as soon as the rain started."

"In case you've forgotten," the inspector had said coldly, "Miss Dilworth was with me when I found the body, so there's a rather valid reason for her prints to be in both places—as mine are. Perhaps you'd like to put us both on the list of suspects?"

It had been unnecessarily sarcastic, and it still rankled. If anybody made Grace Dilworth a motif tie, Terrizi thought resentfully, they should put on a big foot *and* a gun.

The inspector had located Martha Teague; she was just winding up a class in weaving, if *winding up* was the proper term to describe it. Martha had both sturdy arms held straight up in the air, with what resembled a giant cat's cradle holding her in like a new kind of strait jacket. Even Houdini would have had trouble extricating himself. "Let your instinct be your guide," she was saying. "Let color rush out in all kinds of surprising ways. If you want to change a pattern, do it. So many of us want to change the pattern of our lives, but we're afraid. But with loomless weaving, you needn't be afraid. You make your pattern up as you go along."

The lecture was over, but the pupils had crowded around Martha Teague to ask questions, perhaps with the aim of clarifying confusion and pinning her down while she was still freeing herself from the cat's cradle.

The inspector was thankful to see Terrizi coming down the corridor. Cravenly, by pulling rank, he made the sergeant go into the hassle of ladies and pluck Mrs. Teague away.

Upstairs in her tiny office there was only one extra chair, so Terrizi roamed out to the lobby while the inspector conducted the interview, or tried to. Lucy's remark that Martha Teague's braids were woven into her brains seemed particularly apt at the moment. Given a question, Martha took it into her ardent grasp and wove a dizzying maze.

"Of course my footprints were down there. I went down before the concert started. I had a rain hat, and I'd deliberately come early because I wanted to study those horrible pieces of sculpture close to and see what could be done to keep them from hurting anybody. All those sharp points—and now you can see I was right. I hear they pierced right through that man when he fell on them. I'd told him at the board meeting, when I first saw the photograph of the other one—the one called 'Moon God,' children would get hurt on that thing. He became very unpleasant, said we weren't planning a sculpture garden for children. As if that would keep them out."

The inspector was almost stupefied from boredom, when he sensed a change in her tone. The wooliness fell away, and what came out next had a personal, somber directness. "My youngest grandchild was visiting me and I told her not to play near some rusty old bedsprings behind a neighbor's shed. So of course she and the other children bounced on them and a rusty wire pierced her right eye, and she'll be blind in that eye for life. I blamed myself for not watching her, and my son and daughter-in-law blamed me even more. The whole thing nearly broke my heart. I was in such a state I stopped going to church and I didn't want to see anybody, but Alec Foster persuaded me to come to the craft classes, and I tell you, they saved my life. I know Mrs. Ramsdale makes fun of the classes—once I heard her going on to Alec about amateurs—but she's an artist and she can be creative any old time. She doesn't know what it's like to be so frustrated and depressed that you feel as if you're weighted down with stones, and then you get that wonderful liberated feeling when you find you can create with your own two hands. It's incredibly satisfying—at least, it satisfies *me*, and that's the important thing."

Oddly enough, the inspector could imagine Lucy saying, Martha's right.

". . . and this Center meant too much to me to have that Davin Lowry ruin it with his peculiar notions. I thought at first he was charming and that he really cared about the arts, and then at the meeting I realized he cared more about himself than anything else, and he didn't care who got hurt. He was horrid to Alec, and horrid about children, and I just got so steamed up I decided I'd fix those statues of his without his knowing anything about it."

"How?" McDougal got that in fast.

"I thought I'd knit little mitts the color of those sharp metal prongs and slide them on both pieces sometime when nobody was looking, and that would blunt them enough so a child wouldn't get her eye poked out. And if Miss Dilworth and that man found out and fired me, at least it would be better than their firing Alec."

The cigarette McDougal had lit tasted so awful—like lighted mattress stuffing—that he wanted to put it out, but he couldn't see an ashtray. The only thing remotely resembling one had paper clips in it.

"Just dump them out," Martha said. He decided she was more observant than she seemed. "Alec gave up smoking, so I took away the ashtrays because they'd just remind him."

He was tired of hearing about people doing things to make life easier for Alec. Even to the extent of murder?

"Did you get the impression Lowry wanted to fire Alec?"

"I wouldn't have put it past him. I heard them talking in Alec's office after the meeting, and I could tell Alec was dreadfully upset. He sounded so—well, so emotional."

"Could you hear what they said?"

Martha Teague looked regretful. "I might have, but Mrs. Voorhies came in just then to show me a tray she's painting, and she has a rather carrying voice, so I couldn't hear above that. Something about 'no place to discuss this now.' That was Mr. Lowry—he sounded very unfriendly. And of course I wouldn't wish anybody to fall down those terrible stairs, but as long as he did, I think it's a judgment."

Her eyes, in that doughy round face under the crown of braids, were glittering bright. "Alec would have been utterly miserable if that man had lived. He's had enough trouble in his life without any more."

McDougal was about to say, "You mean his sister?" when Martha swept on. "If two friends want to share a house and do congenial things together, I think it's disgusting for people in this town to make jokes behind their backs or wrinkle up their noses. After all, some of their own children take drugs and steal things and drive a hundred and ten miles an hour and kill innocent people on the highway, and nobody acts as if *they're* pariahs. But two nice, harmless men who are always thoughtful and kind—when I was in bed with a strep throat Bert Melton made me pineapple custard and Alec came in every day to bring things and cheer me up—well, you can't make *me* believe they're mentally ill—oh, Alec, we were just talking about you. What did you do to your hand?"

Alec Foster was flushed, and he gave an impression of panting as if he'd been running. He thrust both hands into the pockets of his jacket. "Had to tear out some underbrush around the terrace before we laid more bricks."

McDougal, conjuring up an instant picture of Foster's side yard as he'd seen it that morning, couldn't remember any underbrush close to the house. "You were at home working on the terrace this afternoon?" He didn't add, While a sergeant and two detectives were looking for you? but the implication hung in the air.

"It was last night before the concert," Alec said quickly. "I needed some occupational therapy as an antidote to coping with the pianist. She's the arpeggio type with a temperament to match."

"Is that why you didn't drive her back to the Inn after the concert?"

"No." A very bare word; without accompaniment, it rang out loud as a gong. Alec was standing with his feet apart, and his underlip stuck out defiantly.

"If we could go into your office, there are some points I'd like to clear up." Remembering that Martha Teague's cubicle was within hearing range, probably even with the door between the offices closed, the inspector added, "Mrs. Teague, thank you for sparing me time. If you'd like to go back to your class now. . . ."

"Oh, I'm through with that for the day."

Alec said, "Martha, would you run Mrs. Voorhies home? She

sniffed gold leaf and was out for the count. I'd rather entrust her to you."

Martha pulled open the top drawer of her desk. "I wish I'd known earlier. I have some smelling salts right here."

As the two men walked into the adjoining office, McDougal caught a strong reek of whisky emanating from his companion. Alec said fliply, "Martha's the only girl I know who keeps smelling salts in her drawers. You'd be surprised how handy it is."

The flipness made McDougal bear down even harder than he might have. "You knew Lowry was dead before the janitor phoned you this morning."

"I did not. But of course my saying it doesn't convince you. I think I'll break over and have a cigarette, if I may cadge one from you, Inspector."

McDougal held out his pack of Kents in the manner of one who may snatch it back any second, like an inquisitor taunting a prisoner. He did let Alec extract a cigarette, but he didn't offer to light it. Alec had to ask for a match.

"There are things Melton could have told me about your activities last evening, but he refused. He said I must ask you."

Alec took a deep puff. "Lord, I should have held onto Martha's smelling salts myself. One drag and I'm whirling like a top." He went on, "I'm tougher than Bert, Inspector. Tell me what you want to know, and if it's any of your business, I'll tell you."

"When somebody is murdered, anything is my business."

"Bert told me it was murder."

"And now tell me why you made an assignation with Davin Lowry at the Center last night."

"I resent your calling it an 'assignation.' And what we discussed is entirely my business. If necessary, I'll get a lawyer to defend my rights."

McDougal was annoyed at himself, and dismayed, for not having delivered the customary warning. He said stiffly, "I'm sorry. I should have brought that up sooner. But you aren't helping yourself by this chip-on-the-shoulder attitude."

"If you want to lock me up, go ahead. I assume even you will allow me to phone a lawyer from jail. I don't plan to wither away there indefinitely like Mario."

"Mario's been released long ago." Four hours seemed very long ago indeed, the day dragging wearily along after the almost sleepless night. But through the fog of tiredness, McDougal saw that Alec was reacting strangely to the news of Mario's release. He looked astonished, then speculative, as if he were thinking, What's in it for me?

"Mario had the sense to tell us everything he knew."

"And I have too much sense. Let's leave it at that for now. And I'm not as drunk as Mario was, Inspector. I had two stiff whiskies a while ago, but I'm painfully sober. I should have had four or five."

"Where were you after you got back from the airport—till now? That's almost two hours."

"I went home to have lunch. Bert had made my favorite cold cucumber soup."

"You didn't answer your phone. And when Sergeant Terrizi went by your house around three thirty, nobody was there."

"I must have been on the way back here."

"It wouldn't take you an hour to drive three miles into Wingate."

"I was held up downstairs. I came in the back way and stopped when I saw Mrs. Voorhies laid out. She's the one who's been sniffing gold leaf. She paints with her nose."

"Both the sergeant and I were downstairs for at least twenty minutes and you weren't there."

Alec smiled blandly. "I can't think how we missed each other."

"You and Lowry didn't miss each other last night."

For the first time, Alec's liquor-induced bravado faded. He looked frightened and ill. "We had a private matter to settle."

"Because you'd learned he was with your sister's husband before she killed herself?"

"Leave my sister out of this," Alec almost shouted. Then, with a shrug, "Sorry, Inspector, I sound like a southern redneck: 'The sacredness of a pure woman.' But you're on the wrong track. I can't discuss this any further."

133

"You were trying to blackmail Lowry."

Alec said with contempt, "Lucy should hear you say that."

McDougal felt so boxed in he said, "It's typical of a homosexual to try to hide behind a woman's skirts."

"And it's typical of you to think that way. Most police officers do."

That stung. "We're out to catch a murderer—not to pass moral judgment."

Alec said, more to himself, "My sister met her husband through me. It still haunts me."

"Enough so you'd kill, evidently."

"Whatever happened to that old saw, 'A man is innocent until proven guilty'? It used to be as American as apple pie. Except, of course, when police use blackmail themselves on a homosexual prisoner, or beat him into a phony confession. Don't try that with me, Inspector."

McDougal, who had never rubber-hosed even so much as a target dummy, said something that sounded regrettably like, "I wouldn't dirty my hands on you."

"You'd be sorry if you did. Bert Melton, believe it or not, was heavyweight champion in college. And he's a deeply loyal friend." As if to himself, Alec muttered, "More than he should be."

12

Lucy was doing her facial exercises while she stirred the beef dish. Usually, she got them over with briskly in the morning in her bedroom, but the morning after a murder there simply hadn't been time. Or if there'd been time, there hadn't been the inclination; she had been in a mood to sag. It had seemed more curative to bake the apple spice bread and take McDougal his breakfast and prepare the anchovy-and-onion filling for the tarts, and sketch birds which turned out to be Davin Lowry because he kept stalking through her mind. Now, soon after five o'clock, she was doing her exercises with a special vigor heightened by annoyance. The first exercise consisted of sticking out her tongue as far as it would go—a *yanh, yanh, yanh* effect. This prevented the jaw from sagging, or so it was alleged, and it seemed to have worked quite well. In the second exercise, she bared her teeth fiercely, like wolf fangs; this looked nasty but was supposed to be firming to cheeks, prevent lines around the mouth, and something or other else Lucy couldn't remember but which she believed was all to the good.

She was doing the two exercises alternately while she stirred with a wooden spoon and fumed about Fred Thorndike's not showing up. She had been alone the entire afternoon, from just after two. Unlike Thoreau, who needed a broad margin around his life, Lucy wanted each page, each day's leaf, crammed to the edges with talk and work and good meals and loving, lively attention. To have given up her Thursday afternoon stint at the Thrift Shop, which was always a good, gossipy session with tea thrown in, made her all the crosser at Fred. When she'd considered him as a murderer, he had seemed interesting, if slightly repellent. She'd been looking forward to hearing his inside story, although she'd taken the precaution of having her siren flashlight handy as well as her manicure scissors. The scissors were to jab him, if necessary. And after all this exciting buildup, pleasured by the thought that she'd be clearing Alec Foster and pulling off a coup that would stun the inspector, to have a dull, empty, lonely afternoon was a thudding anticlimax. She hadn't even had a new murder mystery on hand because the paperback one she thought was new she found she had already read under another title.

Grace had come back at five and should have had the decency to stop and have a cup of tea with her hostess, but Grace had refused, saying she wanted to shower and dress; you'd think she might have shown a little gratitude. All very well for her to dash upstairs to get all gussied up for the inspector—Lucy approved of that—but her guest could just as easily have showered and dressed at home and come back in time to be sociable.

All the fuming hostess needed right now, in a chain of frustrations, was to have the inspector call and say he was too busy to come home to eat. Then she'd be stuck with the sad, withdrawn fiancée of a dead man, and a beautiful dinner gone to waste. Going *yanh, yanh, yanh* with her tongue expressed how she felt.

The tongue drew in contemplatively as she wondered if the reason Fred hadn't turned up was because he'd been arrested for murder. In that case, the least Fred could have done was to call her. Like that Cole Porter song—Miss Otis regrets she's unable to lunch today. Lucy began to be furious at the inspector for holding the killer incommunicado and not letting her know. Her tongue shot out like an asp's, firming up her fury along with her jawline.

The inspector would have been happy if he'd had any tangible reason, like reporting the arrest of a murderer, to call her. He hadn't enough evidence yet to arrest Alec Foster, much as he wanted to do it for angry, too-personal reasons. He was determined to build up an airtight case, to prove to Lucy (and himself) that prejudice had no part in this. And something about the conversation with Alec, however unpleasant it had been, had twanged his instincts as a long-time cop: go slow . . . look into Fred Thorndike a bit more, first.

The "old Thorndike place," as it was known locally, was four miles outside Wingate, and McDougal drove there around five on his way back to Lucy's. The mailbox down at the road was painted fresh white, with THORNDIKE lettered in black and a reflector on top to pick up car lights after dusk. On an impulse, McDougal stopped his car there first, long enough to open the box and peer in. Several letters or bills, and two magazines: *Life* and *Architectural Forum*. The carrier for that route reached Lucy's between three thirty and four, so that meant the mail had probably been delivered between two and two thirty at Fred's. Check that with the post office. Thorndike not only wasn't answering his phone; he hadn't even picked up his mail.

The brass knocker on the front door was roughened with age, but well polished. McDougal thumped it and heard the reverberation echo emptily inside. The big, square house looked as if it had been built in layers like a cake, with the widow's walk on top for frosting. It was a faded white, not actually peeling, but the paint looked somehow thin-blooded. The acre or so of lawn in front needed mowing; the grass came up above the hooves of the antique iron deer on the lawn. McDougal, remembering Fred Thorndike had landscaped the grounds at the Dilworth Center with the symmetry of bush against bush, and birdbath to balance sundial, was rather surprised at the difference here: beautiful, huge old maple and ash trees; wisteria hanging like Spanish moss near the porch that curved out and around in what must once have been called a veranda. The bushes had obviously been clipped, but they weren't planted in symmetrical formation; they sprawled in a profusion of clumps. If Fred Thorndike's ancestors had been heartily in favor of overabundance, steak and pie for breakfast, and five bushes where one would do, it seemed to the inspector the current owner had too much respect for—or fear of—the past to interfere with the prodigality. Or perhaps Fred hadn't had the money to fix things up, and just pottered and puttered with makeshift repairs, plugging the leak in the Thorndike. (The inspector disliked puns, or claimed he did, but every now and then one wriggled into his head.) For a man like Fred who was determined to hang onto this albatross of a family legacy, Grace Dilworth's money would come in handy.

Thinking of Grace, McDougal looked at his watch and realized she'd be expecting him to interview her now, at Lucy's. He decided to go to the studio first for a quick shave and shower.

Afterwards he put on his cream linen jacket and tan gabardine slacks, and this refurbished image in the mirror invigorated him enough so that his eyeballs didn't feel nearly as gritty. His mind sorted out the immediate business and picked the things he wanted to ask Grace about last night.

When he left the studio, he took the short-cut path to the kitchen and was about to call out through the screen door when he stopped in astonishment. Lucy was standing over the stove, stirring something and baring her teeth in a hideous grimace. While the inspector watched, bemused, she next stuck her tongue out at least two inches. This latter expression of loathing was, if anything, more ominous than the first. Had the dish she was cooking turned out to be hopelessly bad?

He retreated a few paces from the screen door and considered. Lucy in a rage was nothing to run into head on, but Lucy in a rage because her dinner was spoiled was something he'd never encountered and didn't want to. As he was debating whether to go around to the terrace and find Grace Dilworth, a mosquito nibbled his cheek, and he slapped it.

Lucy instantly whirled around and called out, "Mac? Where the hell have you been? What have you done with Fred Thorndike?"

The inspector came into the kitchen, carefully averting his gaze from whatever it was on the stove that had turned out so disastrously, and said he'd had people looking for Thorndike off and on all afternoon. "And I just came from there myself."

This deflected Lucy's wrath, at least from the inspector. "I hate to tell you, but I'm afraid he's gone on the lam. He must have killed Davin, and he was supposed to come back and tell me, but he never showed up."

"Are you talking about Fred?" Grace was standing in the doorway from the living room. It was the first time McDougal had seen her in a dress, and she looked much more attractive, more feminine, than she had the night before. The white linen sheath showed off her tanned bare arms and legs. Too many tall women, when they wore sleeveless dresses, had arms that hung down like an orangoutang's; McDougal noted with approval that Grace's tapered in nicely to slim, strong fingers. Her face, without any make-up except a touch of lipstick, was the color of honey, instead of that marble whiteness of shock. She came on into the kitchen. "I called Fred after I left here, and he said he'd come over and see me before he came to see Lucy, but he never showed up. It's so odd, because his car's in my garage. At least, it looks like his car. I noticed it a little while ago, and I thought he must have left it for me to use until I get the Mercedes back." She winced. "Not that I care if I ever see the Mercedes again."

McDougal went to the kitchen phone to call Sergeant Terrizi and give orders on having Thorndike's car examined: "Fingerprints, samples of dust or dried mud, test for bloodstains. Search the house and grounds. If you find anything, call me back at Mrs. Ramsdale's." There were no trains in or out of Wingate; the only bus went through town around noon; if Thorndike's car was sitting in Grace's garage, he wasn't apt to have got away. But as a precaution McDougal asked to have a description of Fred broadcast over the police short-wave. "And sergeant, check the car-rental agencies."

When he hung up, Grace said, "I couldn't help hearing what you said, and it made me wonder. Because my maid said a detective found the sculpture slides in the back of a bureau drawer in the guest room. So that means Davin didn't go in to the Center to get the slides. He must have gone to meet someone. He was murdered, wasn't he?" She no longer looked tanned and rested; she looked haunted.

"Mac, get her a drink. Get us all a drink. I'll take Grace out to the terrace. She needs air. It's hot as hell in here."

When the inspector came out carrying a tray of drinks, Lucy was saying, "So you see, dear, it wasn't your fault at all. Taking out the steps down to the garden wouldn't have helped, because if somebody wanted to commit murder they'd just think of another method."

McDougal had brought Grace a two-ounce slug of straight Scotch, and she took half of it in one gulp before she said, "But why should anybody want to kill Davin? Nobody around here even *knew* him. Who did he meet in the garden?"

McDougal put down his own drink. "Alec Foster admits he talked to Lowry there after the concert."

"Oh." It was more a small sound of pain. "Davin wanted so much to make Alec understand his job wasn't in danger. He said if he talked to Alec alone . . . but Alec was so bitter and hostile. He must not have believed anything Davin said. How *could* he do it?" She brushed a hand across her cheek. "It's impossible. Alec would never do that."

Lucy, who had kept miraculously quiet for at least one minute, said, "I agree completely with Grace. It must have been Fred. He was acting terribly odd this afternoon. He was missing some of his buttons. Oh, hell! There goes the oven timer. Don't say anything interesting till I come back." She disappeared at a fast trot, remembering to lift the latch so the screen door didn't stick.

The inspector thought irritably, This isn't a coffee klatch, and was about to go right ahead and question Grace when she said, "Isn't Lucy marvelous? When I'm around her I feel like one of the olden time Olympic runners, as if she'd passed along the torch to me and I have to keep going no matter what. And she never even mentions her heart trouble."

"What heart trouble?"

"Oh, I thought you knew. Don't let her know I said anything about it or she'd be furious at me. She had a bad coronary two years ago. We have the same doctor—Morey Halloran—and I know he fusses about her being so hyperactive."

It was all news to McDougal, and such disquieting news that for a minute it knocked everything else out of his head.

"That's why I didn't call her last night when I wanted to borrow her car."

The inspector came to attention; this was one of the points that had puzzled him. "I knew she had a phone by her bed, and I was afraid being roused from sleep so suddenly at two A.M. would be too much of a shock." Grace shook her head ruefully. "And instead I gave her an even worse shock, when she heard me in the garage. I told her today that my father used to say she had ears like a fox."

"You were the one who had the worst shock of all." McDougal's voice was gentle. "Can you bear to talk about it a little?"

"Now that I know it's murder, I want to do everything I can to help you."

It was what he'd counted on her to say, but to have her live up to the impression he'd formed was freshly gratifying. "Did you know, for instance, that Davin Lowry tried to see Lucy last night? And do you know why?"

"Oh, yes. I've already explained that to Lucy." Grace repeated the gist of the earlier conversation. "I knew Lucy would make him realize that when two people love each other as we did, it isn't important which one has more money. I could just have divided up everything and given us each half."

This too seemed to McDougal an admirable indication of her character.

"And Davin was so totally unlike a gigolo. He was very strong and forthright and—and protective." Her voice almost broke, but she made herself go on. "I'm sure that's why he must have gone back to the Center last night. He knew I'd been upset about some of the attitudes at the board meeting. Especially Alec's. Although I hate to say that now, because I still can't believe Alec would do anything so horrible. Or Fred either—although I'd never seen Fred so worked up as he was yesterday. But if Alec admits meeting Davin there last night—and they had talked a minute or so in the afternoon, in Alec's office. Davin went there when I went to find the janitor. So they could have arranged, then, to meet later. At dinner, Davin said, 'Alec is running the Center for amateurs, and it needs a more professional tone, but that needn't jeopardize his job. If he could just be made to understand that.' And so Davin must have tried again to reassure Alec, and if he hadn't gone in to meet him, he'd still be alive."

Put that way, it sounded, even to the inspector, like too simplified a conclusion. He disliked being rushed into decisions; and Fred, by disappearing, had complicated matters. "Just because Foster admits meeting Lowry, that doesn't mean he killed him. Fred Thorndike had even more reason to be jealous."

He liked the matter-of-fact way Grace nodded, without any of the coyness most women would have shown at the mention of a jealous admirer.

"We found Fred Thorndike's footprints down in the garden, so he was definitely there during the evening. The rain didn't start till around seven."

"I remember," Grace said somberly. "I could hardly pull Davin away when it started raining, because he was so excited about getting the two pieces out of the crates and setting them up. Just to give me a rough idea of the way he'd planned the layout. He'd wanted 'Moon God' right away too—those three pieces were his favorites—but 'Moon God' was still in the show in New York, and the gallery owner didn't want us to take it till the show was over." She closed her eyes, then opened them and said rather defiantly, "I'm going ahead with the sculpture garden as a memorial. I've already told Lucy."

"Please don't tell anyone else. I mean that. Not till the murderer's safely locked up."

"But Fred already knows. Lucy told him. He mentioned it this afternoon—I mean, on the phone. He sounded so angry."

The inspector swore. "From now on, don't leave here alone without letting me know. Don't even go home to pick something up—clothes or whatever—without police protection. It's lucky you didn't see Thorndike when he came this afternoon."

"I was still so full of sedatives, or at least the hangover from the sedative the doctor gave me last night, that I lay down on the bed in my room and actually fell asleep again. So I didn't even hear Fred's car come in, or hear him knock. I guess I'm still in a kind of daze."

Lucy was back with a plate of tiny, hot, anchovy-and-onion tarts. "You have every right to feel dazed, dear, and you didn't eat any breakfast or lunch. So we're going to have our first course right now, with our next drink."

The inspector told himself he should go over and see how Terrizi and the men were making out next door. Several cars had already pulled in over there. But then he told himself that the sergeant would phone as soon as there was anything to report. In the meantime, he might as well have a wee tart and another drink; he felt he'd earned that small respite, after going thirty-six hours with almost no sleep.

He had seven wee tarts. Even Grace ate several, and she seemed much more animated, responding to the inspector in that indefinable way another woman senses. It was exactly what Lucy had wanted and plotted for, but now that she'd brought it off, she felt oddly shut out and superfluous. Grace had asked McDougal whether a mobile crime lab was useful. "I know the police in New York have at least one. There was a burglary in our apartment building there and the mobile unit came within minutes. Sam—my father—was very impressed by the speed and efficiency. He said Wingate ought to have something like that. I wondered what you thought about it."

McDougal said it would be a great help, but that the Wingate police couldn't even get money for a new headquarters they needed badly, much less a mobile crime lab.

"I hadn't realized. I've been so selfishly wrapped up in my own life. But Sam left me so much money, and I want to do more with it. I mean, more than just helping the arts. If you'd advise me sometime. . . ."

Lucy thought wryly, Nothing like a million dollars to grease a woman's path to the next love.

The inspector said he'd be delighted to give Grace any advice he could. He went into some detail about the cumbersome current procedure involved in rounding up detectives and experts, gathering evidence, and sending it off to a lab. "Sometimes we have to send it clear up to state headquarters in Hartford. On the casts of those footprints, for example. . . ."

Grace seemed fascinated; McDougal was talking more than Lucy had ever heard him. She was surprised he hadn't gone right off to join Terrizi, but she was of two minds about that. The beef bourguignon for dinner was probably the best she'd ever made, and she wanted full appreciation. And Mac wouldn't have had a decent meal since breakfast.

Neither of the absorbed twosome noticed when Lucy left them to toss the salad and warm the garlic bread. She came back ten minutes later and said rather sharply, "Mac, you forgot to open the wine ahead," which was a bit unfair because she hadn't even told him they were having wine. She remembered, belatedly, something else she hadn't told him: Flora Pollit had left a message saying the inspector must call her at once because it was of the Utmost Urgency. Probably wanted to tell him not to pollute the earth by burying mothballs. Lucy shrugged; Flora could wait. "Dinner's ready and I don't want to have it dry up. The beef bourguignon is perfect right now."

McDougal had poured the wine and was lifting his fork for a taste of the much-touted beef dish when Sergeant Terrizi burst in through the terrace door and raced to the dinner table at the back end of the living room. "Excuse me, but some Brownie Scouts are outside, Inspector, and I thought you'd want to see them."

It was a tribute to his innate faith in the sergeant that McDougal, who had never felt drawn to Brownie Scouts, even in the abstract, instantly put down his fork and went out.

There were five or six of the little creatures in brownish uniforms; they looked like a gathering of elves. A child who wasn't much taller than McDougal's knees stepped forward and gasped, "Mother's down in the woods with our dog and she sent us to tell you there's a dead man in the blackberry bushes and she'll stay on guard but please hurry because she's a little nervous."

13

In the glare of portable searchlights, McDougal's shadow loomed above the bushes tall as a telephone pole. The police doctor said, "If you expect me to jump into the brambles to examine the body, then get me a suit of armor. And my wife says why can't you have any daylight murders for a change? More wholesome." But he went down on one knee, soberly, intently, when the body was laid on a large flat rock beside the stream. Two state troopers, wearing heavy gauntlets, had carried it out of the bushes.

"He was struck from behind. No puncture. Probably knocked out with the first blow, but it took more of a pounding than that to cause death. Funny, he's got sand in his hair and on his jacket. Poor Fred, always curried himself like a horse. Looks as if he may have died of cerebral hemorrhage, but I can't be sure of that till I do the autopsy." He went on probing.

"Can you give us an idea of when he died?"

"You know, these politicians I always see interviewed on TV—whenever they're asked something that might get them into a jam, they just clamp their lips in a genial smile and say, 'Gentlemen, no comment.'"

"We won't quote you to the press. Come on, make a wild guess."

"Well, *rigor mortis* is already setting in. I'd guess six or seven hours ago."

"Between two and three o'clock this afternoon," Sergeant Terrizi muttered.

"You do the subtracting. I've got enough problems."

McDougal was doing a quick timetable in his head. "Miss Dilworth said she talked to Thorndike on the phone around two thirty, and he was supposed to see Lucy Ramsdale soon after that, but he didn't show up."

The doctor grunted. "I'll bet Lucy screamed to high heaven about being stood up. She likes people to dance to her tune. This guy won't dance to anybody's tune now, except maybe a choir of angels if you believe in that guff. Me, the idea of life everlasting makes me groan. Four score and ten or twenty's enough. Not that Fred Thorndike got his fair share. He wasn't more than fifty. Thought he and Grace might hit it off after the fiancé was killed —wow, she's lost two guys in twenty-four hours. Does she know about this one yet?"

"No, and she should." The inspector found he was wishing he could go back and tell her himself. She had been touchingly grateful for his help the night before, and he was beginning to fancy himself in the role of strong male support.

Terrizi's shadow moved closer, and against McDougal's it looked like a ping-pong paddle. "How come she didn't see Thorndike when he drove to her house? She was over there all afternoon."

"She was still groggy from the shot of sedative. She's not used to barbiturates." For McDougal, it was one more point in her favor. "She slept most of the afternoon."

The sergeant said stubbornly, "Thorndike didn't just hit himself over the head and stagger down here from her house and collapse in the thicket."

McDougal thought of Grace Dilworth's strong slim arms and the long, tanned fingers. She was probably big enough, and fit enough, to carry the body of a small man down here to the blackberry bushes. But it wasn't Grace who'd had scratches all over her hands. He took a cold satisfaction in telling the sergeant about Foster's weak excuse for the scratched hands. "Get Sibley to check with the barracks on his two-way radio. They may have some word from the lab on prints on the car."

The sergeant went off briskly and came back several minutes later at a funereal pace. Even his voice was dragging. "Foster's fingerprints are on the steering wheel with Thorndike's."

"So if he drove the car over to Grace's after he killed Thorndike. . . . That terrace he's building is littered with sandbags, loose sand, cement—*and a wheelbarrow*. That may be how he got the body down here." He raised his voice. "Carlin!" The small, plump detective who had been searching the ground around the blackberry bushes came panting. In the woods setting, with his hair disheveled and his dark-circled eyes magnified by the searchlight, he looked more than ever like a raccoon. McDougal was pleased he'd remembered the man's name. "Carlin, will you see if there's any sort of path going up through the woods in that direction?" He pointed toward Foster's house. "If there is, look for the track of a wheelbarrow. There should be clear markings if it carried a dead body. And get casts of any footprints. A man's shoe—small—is my guess."

Carlin went bouncing off.

Sergeant Terrizi muttered, "There used to be a path from the Dilworths' house that came down here and curved on over through the woods."

It was probably just as well that the inspector didn't hear him. "We'll take samples of the sand on the jacket and compare it with scrapings from Foster's terrace. There ought to be some flakes of powdered cement."

The sergeant had drifted off with a portable searchlight and found that the path up to Grace's house was still there, all right, but it showed no trace of a wheelbarrow's deep groove. He returned to the center of attention—the dead body—feeling self-chastened.

Carlin yelled, "Yeah, Inspector, you were right. Sibley's getting the prints. Want I should follow the track and see where it comes out?"

"Yes. But don't go up as far as Foster's house yet. I want to be along. Sergeant, will you go back to Mrs. Ramsdale's and tell them we've found Thorndike—dead. Then meet me at Foster's."

The police doctor was raising one of the dead man's stiffened arms as if he were arranging a clothes dummy in a display window. "Snagged place here on the sleeve. May have caught the jacket on thorns when the body was dumped in."

McDougal had just delegated a trooper to examine the blackberry bushes for any scrap of cloth when Raccoon-eyes trotted back. "We found the wheelbarrow. It was left in the woods, but the track goes on up toward Foster's house, so he must have brought the body down that way. And here's some threads were caught on a splinter in the wheelbarrow." He handed a plasticine envelope to McDougal, who knelt beside the body, elated. If the threads matched—and the sand—then he'd have Foster cold. The threads matched the sleeve exactly.

As McDougal got up, he saw Terrizi still standing there, looking as if he wanted to say something. "Yes, Sergeant? I thought you'd left five minutes ago." He knew he was sounding too curt, but he was annoyed.

The sergeant had thought of one other point, but now that he had a chance to speak he dreaded rousing the inspector's wrath again. "Uh—it can wait."

"Then get cracking."

Lucy, sitting on the terrace with Grace, had given up trying to stifle her yawns. She was still exasperated at McDougal's rushing off without dinner. All he'd said was that the Brownie Scouts had run into some trouble down in the woods and he and Terrizi wanted to investigate. Trust Janie Trask to send for an inspector to extricate her Brownies from a briar patch or poison ivy or whatever. I should have given Mac a box lunch to take along, she thought sourly.

Grace had barely touched her beef bourguignon, just pushed it around politely with her fork and said, "Delicious." Lucy had noted, and resented, the difference in her guest as soon as the inspector had left: she was no longer animated and talkative—she gave off the negative rays of a woman who's waiting for something more interesting to happen and won't expend effort on present company in the meantime. Lucy felt ashamed of her uncharitable thoughts when Grace said, "Last night at this time, Davin and I were having a brandy and making such wonderful plans. I'd never been so happy."

Lucy made sympathetic noises. "Did the sketch fit into the frame?"

"What sketch?" Grace's voice was vague, wandery.

Her hostess seethed. "The sketch I made of Davin."

"Oh! Oh, it fits perfectly. Darling Lucy, it's the most wonderful thing you could possibly have given me. I'll never be parted from it."

But you didn't bother to bring it back with you, Lucy thought grumpily. She gave another, more jawbreakerish, yawn.

Grace said sweetly, "If you're tired, why don't you go to bed now? I'll wait a little longer for the inspector and find if he's had any word of Fred. And didn't he say he was going to see Alec?"

That roused Lucy like a cold washcloth flung in her face. Alec's admitting he'd met Davin late at the Center troubled her all over again. And it was odd that neither Alec nor Bert had called or come over all evening. But if they thought they'd run into the inspector here, she didn't blame them for staying away. She heard a faint crackle and sat up straight. "Somebody's coming up from the woods."

She felt suddenly cheered and hospitable. Poor Mac. She could warm up the bourguignon and give him a good meal. When Terrizi's stocky figure emerged from a clump of trees, Lucy was so let down she took it out on the sergeant. "You shouldn't have let the inspector stay down there. He hasn't had any dinner."

Neither have I, the sergeant said silently. It was the first time Mrs. Ramsdale hadn't offered him something to eat or drink, and he attributed this cool reception to Grace Dilworth's being there. Seeing her sitting on the terrace had flicked a raw spot: so all right, he'd been suspicious of the wrong person, but the inspector shouldn't have jumped on him for speaking his mind. Young cops should be encouraged to think for themselves. He said in a flat tone, "Inspector McDougal sent me to tell you we found Fred Thorndike down in the woods. Or the Trasks' dog found him. He's dead."

"In the *woods*," Grace said. "How did he get there?"

Terrizi heard her with half an ear because Lucy was making shocked sounds and then talking at the same time. "Maybe it was the easiest way out—to kill himself."

"He was murdered, ma'am. Somebody took the body down there in a wheelbarrow."

"From where?" Lucy said sharply.

"They've followed the track almost to Mr. Foster's place."

Lucy's throat tightened so that it was hard to swallow, and her heart pounded erratically.

"Then it was Alec who killed Davin." Grace was brushing her hand across her cheek in agitation. "I still can't believe it. After all I've done for him."

Anger lubricated Lucy's vocal cords. "He's done more for that Center than you've ever done for him. You were lucky to get him."

The sergeant looked at her with affection, cheering to himself, Thatta girl.

Grace was hurt, but gentle. "Lucy dear, you've had a bad shock. You don't know what you're saying. You're defending a murderer."

"I'm defending a friend. And we still don't know he's a murderer." Her voice rose in a kind of wail. "It doesn't fit. Alec would never have killed Fred. Somebody else did it."

Grace looked startled. "You mean Bert Melton? To cover up the first killing for Alec?"

"Bert's not an imbecile."

"But that unhealthy devotion to each other."

"Oh, bull. Plenty of husbands and wives are devoted. What's so unhealthy about it?"

The sergeant had been swiveling his head from one contestant to the other, following the exchange like a tennis match.

"Sam always said homosexuals weren't to be trusted."

"Sam said a lot of stone-headed things in his time, and that's one of them. I'd trust Bert and Alec with my life. Alec might get mad and give somebody a push, but he'd never have soaped those steps. And Bert's too honest for his own good. He even told one customer that the wormy chestnut commode she wanted to buy had been bored by human worms. And another time—Nicky, why are you coughing like that? Get yourself a cold beer and calm down."

The sergeant said unhappily, "I can't. I'm supposed to meet the inspector over at Foster's right now, and if he finds what he expects. . . ." He didn't have to spell it out. He'd just wanted Mrs. Ramsdale to be prepared for Foster's arrest.

"If Mario got out of jail at noon," Lucy said, thoughtfully, "he could still be a suspect."

The sergeant shuddered. Not that again. And to have the nefarious thought come from Mrs. Ramsdale, of all people. She'd been staunchly on Mario's side until she needed him as a scapegoat.

Grace Dilworth, to his bewilderment, said that suspecting Mario was simply ridiculous. Women!

"Oh, I don't really take him seriously," Lucy said, "but if we have to stall for time, we might as well confuse the issue."

"Not with Mario, you don't. He was home sleeping all afternoon. Angie's mama locked him in his room so's he wouldn't go on another bender." Terrizi devoutly hoped Mario hadn't shinnied down a drainpipe.

"Maybe we dismissed Myra Farmington too soon. I'll give her some thought. And Martha Teague—I'd forgotten about her grandchild . . . Nicky, you tell the inspector he is not to arrest Alec for twenty-four hours. If he does he'll feel like a fool. Will you give him exactly that message?"

"No, ma'am," the sergeant said. "I'd have to emigrate to Australia."

"I think the inspector can be trusted to do his job," Grace said. "He seems to me an exceptionally brilliant police officer. Don't you think so, Sergeant?"

At least Miss Dilworth hadn't called him Nicky. And she was asking very nicely for his opinion. The sergeant said yes, Inspector McDougal was brilliant, all right.

"But he's trying Oscar Wilde," Lucy said darkly.

As he got into his car, the sergeant puzzled over that last remark. Who was Oscar and why was he wild?

14

Angie was watching with satisfaction as the sergeant demolished a pizza the size of a platter. They were sitting in Terrizi's car in front of a small roadside restaurant emblazoned in neon: THE PURPLE PIZZA—Open 4 p.m. to Midnight. A smaller neon sign just below had lost the bulbs in one letter, so that it sent out a somewhat esoteric message: AVAILABLE FOR PRIVATE ARTIES.

The sergeant and his girl weren't having an artie. Faced with the deadline of closing time and a ravening hunger, Terrizi had ordered three king-size pizzas at eleven forty-five. One was for Angie, who nibbled hers around the edges and talked while the sergeant gobbled: "Mr. Foster came to see Uncle Mario late this afternoon, and he went up to his room to talk and they stayed there so long it held up dinner. By the time he left, Mama was spitting nails." This last bit wasn't news; Angie's mama often spit nails, in assorted sizes. "I just got in at the end of it because I'd worked an hour overtime to make up for the hour I took off this morning to go see Uncle Mario in jail."

The sergeant mumbled something through a mouthful of pizza. It would have sounded as incomprehensible as Gullah to the ordinary listener, but not to a girl of Italian blood who was used to hearing men project through the fullness of pasta. "Oh, you needn't worry about that. Mama took away his pants so he couldn't go out this afternoon. I mean, he could have, but he wouldn't have run around town in his shorts."

If the sergeant hadn't had both hands full, as well as his mouth, he'd have embraced his companion for this welcome information. As it was, he emitted an animal grunt expressing relief.

"Uncle Mario wouldn't tell Mama what he and Mr. Foster had talked about, and that made her even madder. She said it wasn't safe to stay up in his room with a pansy."

This time, the sergeant's grunt signified strong disapproval.

"I know. Mama's even worse about Women's Lib. But you should have heard Uncle Mario go after her. He told her Michelangelo and Leonardo da Vinci were homosexuals and mama should be proud they were Italian. And mama said, well, she wasn't proud Mussolini was Italian but at least he had babies."

The sergeant choked strenuously and had to be patted on the back. For so lissome a girl, Angie could whack like a rug beater. "There. Breathe through your nose. You're dribbling mozzarella on your clean uniform."

This time, the sergeant spoke rather clearly. Even a casual passer-by might have understood him to say he didn't give a damn what happened to his uniform.

"Well, your mama does. She's the one who has to wash them."

Not any more, the sergeant said. He was going to resign from the force.

"You're just saying that because you're tired. Inspector McDougal always wants you to work with him because you're *good*. And I'm sure he didn't mean to insult you tonight. He was just thinking of you when he told you to go home and get some sleep."

"He just didn't want to hear what I was trying to tell him as soon as we got to Foster's. But I still say something's screwy because when I told her and Mrs. Ramsdale that Fred Thorndike had been found down in the woods dead, Grace didn't say 'Dead!' She said 'In the *woods!*' Like she already knew he was dead but she couldn't understand how his body had got down there."

"But you can't think she killed her own fiancé! And if she didn't kill *him*, then why should she kill Mr. Thorndike? I mean, it wouldn't even be like a lovers' quarrel. If I killed you, if you were unfaithful or something, I certainly wouldn't run around killing anybody else afterward."

The sergeant said he would never be unfaithful. He put his second pizza back in the bag and proceeded to demonstrate why he felt no real need to stray—or be killed.

Angie was splendidly responsive, until a strand of her long silken hair got caught on the top button of the sergeant's uniform. This injected a certain practical note, and by the time she'd untangled, she was cool as a half-ripe cucumber. "Nicky, I think you're being very unfair to Inspector McDougal. You should have more faith in him. He was so wonderful that time nobody believed me, and he got the right murderer. He sort of switched at the last minute."

"He won't switch this time," the sergeant said gloomily. "Because there's already too much evidence. Foster's fingerprints are on the steering wheel on top of Thorndike's, and he's not even trying to clear himself. When I left them, he was still telling the inspector, 'I know you'll arrest me no matter what I say, so I wish you'd get it over with.'"

Angie sighed. In the glow of neon, her Botticelli face expressed a lovely compassion. "I feel so sorry for the inspector."

That made two people who were sorry for the inspector; the second person was McDougal. As he turned into Lucy's driveway around midnight, he felt like a man who'd been churned in a blender.

Alec Foster had received the police with twitching hostility. He had been advised of his rights and had perversely refused to call a lawyer. "Not yet. Bert will call one for me after you cart me off. Bert had nothing to do with any of this, by the way."

Foster was no longer trying to hide his scratched hands. He rather flaunted them, and Detective Carlin's dark-rimmed eyes followed the short, plump fingers in rolling fascination, as if they were snakes coming out of a basket.

"Yes, I admit I put the body there. But if you came home and found a dead man on your terrace, Inspector, you might have panicked too."

154

"I'd have called the police." McDougal tried to make his voice sound magisterial, but he was too tired for timbre.

"And if I'd called you, would you have believed me? One man dead last night soon after I left him—another one dumped on my terrace today. And me already criminally suspect as a practitioner of 'unnatural acts.' Socrates would have known how I felt."

Bert Melton said, "Don't drag Socrates into this. The inspector's not plying you with hemlock. He's trying to get at the truth, and you're certainly not making it easy."

Melton was wearing the same striped shirt he'd worn that morning, limp now, and he was gray with fatigue, but he still gave off a feeling of solidity and sensible kindness. "Inspector, you look ready to drop. I won't offer you a drink, but if you and Detective Carlin would like coffee and a sandwich, we were just going to have a snack. We didn't get dinner."

Raccoon Eyes looked hopefully at the inspector, who was surprised to hear himself say, "Thank you, we will."

"Well, *I'll* have a drink," Alec said. "The condemned man drank a hearty meal."

Melton said mildly, "You've already had enough on an empty stomach. I'll bring in the coffee."

Alec Foster pouted, but he didn't argue. And he made no move to get himself a drink after Melton went to the kitchen. He even answered the inspector's next question with relative directness: "My fingerprints are on the steering wheel because I drove Thorndike's car away from here. I'm such a boob amateur I didn't even think of wearing gloves. If I'd had any sense, I'd have put the body in the car first and saved myself all that trouble. Lugging a dead man down through the woods in a wheelbarrow is not my idea of a picnic. If he'd been a stranger, I might have felt rather adventurous. But I kept thinking, 'Fred Thorndike would *hate* riding in a wheelbarrow.'"

McDougal was so repelled by the flipness he had to keep himself rigidly under control. "Why pick Miss Dilworth's house to leave the car?"

Alec was silent at first, but his long lashes quivered with the

155

nervous blinking. "Why not? It was one of the nearest houses, and I didn't want to drive Fred's car any distance because I'd be spotted. Besides, I knew you were waiting to interview me, and I'd already used up too much time getting rid of the body."

"Miss Dilworth gave you her father's bicycle after he died; did you ride it into the Center last night?"

Again the blinking. "I most certainly did not." Had there been a slight emphasis on *I?*

"Where is the bicycle now?" A trooper had searched the place earlier and found nothing.

"It was stolen."

"When?"

"I'm not sure. I hadn't ridden it for a while."

"Did you report it as stolen?"

"To the *police?*" Alec grimaced. "Let sleeping pigs lie. Whenever I have to go past headquarters, I cross over to the other side of the street."

"Alec, drop the hippie act. It's obnoxious." Bert Melton had come back with a loaded tray, and he had to bend way over to put it on the low lacquered table, but he managed the balancing act deftly. The inspector was somehow surprised to see that the cups were big pottery mugs and the sandwiches were thick, with the crusts on. "Corned beef," Melton said. "English mustard if you like it." Alec handed around plates; Detective Carlin passed the mustard.

McDougal, in the lightheadedness of exhaustion, thought, Mad Hatter's coffee break, and we have a raccoon instead of a rabbit.

All four men munched quietly for several minutes. The corned beef was lean and good; the coffee was as potently black as the inspector brewed it at home. The fog of tiredness lifted a little; he felt so much better that when Detective Carlin said, "This certainly hits the spot," McDougal would almost have liked to say, "It certainly does." He felt that Melton had shown grace of spirit to be hospitable under these circumstances. And he felt slightly embarrassed to go right back to the questioning and bite the hand that had fed him.

"Mr. Melton, you said Foster was home by eleven and that

you didn't hear him go out again. You said you'd have heard the car go out. But you wouldn't have heard a bicycle, would you?"

"Alec did not go out again." Melton flushed. "I can swear to that."

"For reasons you can guess," Alec said. "But people like us can't come right out and say it."

The inspector was startled to feel an odd sympathy. And a new idea began to shape in his head. If Lowry had been a secret homosexual, a closet fag, and Alec had spotted him as that, then Alec, after what happened to his own sister, would have been determined to prevent its happening to Grace Dilworth. Not using blackmail, but insisting Lowry clear out. And if Lowry refused to leave Grace and her millions. . . .

In quite a gentle tone, he said, "What did you and Lowry talk about in the garden last night?"

"I can't tell you," Alec muttered. "If I did, it would only make things worse for me."

"If Lowry was a homosexual, then what happened to your sister might be happening again, to Grace Dilworth. At least, that's the way you must have reasoned, and I can understand the desperation you felt."

"*You* understand how I felt." It was a jeer.

"I can try if you'll give me some facts to go on. So far, all I have is a massive lot of evidence against you." There was somehow too much of it, the inspector thought suddenly: it was like mountains of food piled on a plate and thrust in front of him. He felt surfeited and at the same time unsatisfied. "If somebody made you the fall guy, then in order to clear you I need your cooperation even more."

"I'm not a stool pigeon. If you're too stupid to figure it out for yourself—"

McDougal got up so abruptly he banged his shin on the coffee table, and the small physical pain intensified his anger. "You're the one who's stupid. You give me no choice but to book you on suspicion of murder."

"Even though I'm innocent. But of course you'd long since rendered the verdict."

"I have tried to give Foster every chance to explain." Mc-Dougal was looking at Bert Melton as he said it. "I hope you believe that."

Melton said, "Oddly enough, I think I do. Alec's been trying to make you lose your temper ever since you came in, and you've been more patient than he deserved. He's behaved with incredible stupidity from the time he found the body on our terrace. He should have called the police, of course, but no homosexual feels absolutely certain he can fling himself into the arms of the law and be protected like any other citizen."

"That aspect never entered into this."

"Perhaps not consciously. But you'd made Alec aware of how much you disliked him, and mistakenly or not, he thought that was the reason."

The inspector was uncomfortably silent.

"That's why I'm presuming to ask a favor of you—let's say to even things up. If you'll hold off arresting Alec, at least for tonight, I'll do my damndest to persuade him to talk. Give us, say, twenty-four hours. I guarantee he won't try to get away. Or if he tries, I'll throw him on the floor and sit on him." Melton managed a tired smile. "That'll squash him, all right."

Somewhat to his own surprise, McDougal had agreed to hold off for twenty-four hours. The fact that Raccoon Eyes obviously disapproved may have contributed to his decision.

Driving home alone, he wondered if he hadn't been remiss in not checking on whether Martha Teague had been at the Center all afternoon. She had said Davin Lowry's death was a "judgment." If she'd been enough unhinged by the accident that blinded her grandchild, she could have passed judgment herself: an eye for an eye, almost literally. She had seemed devoted to Alec, but if she'd gone to his house to find him and had found Fred Thorndike there instead, and Fred had threatened to expose Alec's homosexual tie-up with Lowry, then she might have killed again. She wouldn't have meant to throw suspicion on Alec; quite the contrary. And it would explain Alec's refusing to talk—out of loyalty—till he was surer.

McDougal was so deep in this maze of speculation that he drove past Lucy's mailbox, a half mile too far, and had to turn around in somebody's driveway. His headlights picked up the unknown owner's trash cans lined up beside the driveway, ready for the weekly pickup early the next morning, and the sight of them made him groan. One of his household chores was to put out the trash cans, and he'd forgotten tomorrow was Friday. Maybe Lucy had remembered and wrestled with them herself.

But there were no cans in Lucy's driveway; he'd have to get them out of the garage, and if he pulled up the garage door, Lucy would be bound to hear. She heard everything. She'd come rushing down to find out about Alec, and the inspector couldn't stand the thought of being interrogated right then. The house was dark and silent; let it stay that way.

He turned off his engine and coasted down the last slope of driveway to the studio, then groaned again. Every light in the studio was on, streaming out not in welcome but warningly: Lucy was waiting to corner him.

He turned the doorknob and was surprised to find the door was locked. At least she'd had the sense to shut herself in. He got out his key, turned it in the lock and rattled it angrily as he withdrew it. Let her know how he felt. He was so unprepared for the emptiness of the living room that he was more exasperated than ever. She must be having a nap in his bedroom, of all the gall. But why hadn't she heard him come in? She always claimed, bragged, really, that the slightest sound woke her. But if she couldn't wake up. . . .

McDougal's long legs propelled him down the room in five seconds. The bed was blandly empty; the spread wasn't even wrinkled. Just to make certain, McDougal looked in the closets and in the kitchen. He debated calling the house to make sure Lucy was all right, but if the phone blared by her bed at this hour, it would frighten her. After all, she hadn't been alone in the house: Grace was there in the guest room right across the hall. A good thing for both of them. The thought of that relaxed him so much he yawned and yawned.

He was tempted to sleep in his clothes, but he made himself

undress. As he climbed into his pajama bottoms, a shutter in his mind flipped open; he remembered something that had been said that day by one of the people he'd interviewed. And once he'd remembered that, his mind went racing along. What had been a blocked-off passageway widened out, and the farther he explored it, the surer he felt.

He went to the phone and called the barracks. "I left a patrol car on guard at Foster's so he wouldn't sneak out. Can you spare me another man to guard the rear? It's urgent. I don't want Foster to be on the loose. That goes for Melton too."

He hung up, went into the kitchen again to turn off the light, and saw the note in Lucy's surging scrawl propped on the counter:

Beef Bourguignon in double boiler on stove, on SIM. EAT. Flora Pollit phoned—says you should call her whenever you get in. She'd called earlier but I thought it was mothballs. Now think not but she'll talk your ear off anyway so wait till A.M. Have changed my mind about Grace—she is not the girl for you so don't get interested.
                    Lucy

The inspector made an odd sound, as if he were breathing through a snorkel. He turned off the stove burner, put the top part of the double boiler in the refrigerator, and flicked off the kitchen wall switch. Then, without even brushing his teeth, he got into bed. Mrs. Beeton was still handy, but that night he had no need of her.

15

In this dream of Sergeant Terrizi's, Angie was not a bush; far from it. She was wearing two pizzas like breastplates and lolling on a flat rock in a setting reminiscent of the woods behind Mrs. Ramsdale's when she said, "My slacks zip down the side. Will you help me?"

He had just taken hold of the zipper catch, helpfully, to facilitate action, when some fiend grabbed him by the shoulders. The sergeant struggled fiercely and woke up panting with rage.

When he saw his mother bending over him, Gorgon-headed with curlers, it was like a rerun of a bad movie or the previous morning's awakening. Except that this time his first thought was that his mother had come to tell him, "You can't dream such things till you and Angie are married. A good Catholic girl like that. It's not nice."

To forestall any mind reading or dream analysis he said, "Mama, there's no prowler downstairs and I'm dead tired."

"Jump out of that bed. The inspector wants you."

Terrizi, on reflex, threw off the top sheet ready to leap, then remembered. "Wherever he is, tell him I'm no longer on the case. I'm resigning."

"So you'll be going on welfare. Here's your clean shorts." She turned her back, with maidenly propriety, and went to the closet.

The sergeant saw with some surprise that daylight was filtering in. He looked blearily at his watch; almost six. "Where am I supposed to go this time?" His mother had taken his uniform jacket out of the closet and was examining the top button, frowning. To distract her, he said, "Did somebody else get killed?"

"You'll be next." His mother ostentatiously removed a long, silken dark hair from the jacket button. "Angie's mama should see this."

The sergeant, in the midst of tying his tie, crossed himself hurriedly. "You still haven't told me where the inspector wants me to go."

"I should grill the inspector? Ask him yourself."

"Mama, if I don't know where he is, I can't go there."

"He smokes too much. At least that's one vice you don't have. Put on these clean socks—they match."

"WHERE IS HE?" Terrizi shouted.

"He's dirtying the ashtrays. I already told you."

"You mean he's *here?*"

"Who else's ashtrays would he be using in the breakfast nook? Comb your hair."

Her son combed his hair with his fingers as he ran for the stairs.

Mrs. Terrizi, following minutes later, caught a snatch of the conversation between the two. She was a strong supporter of the theory that all men are little boys at heart, and what she heard only reinforced this conviction: the inspector wanted a bicycle, and her son was saying happily, "Sure. If you wheeled it down through the woods. . . ."

She shrugged tolerantly and asked the inspector how many eggs he'd like for breakfast.

"One."

"One! Nicky has three."

"Then I'll have three," the inspector said expansively.

Lucy heard the bang, thump, grinding sounds she'd been waiting for; the garbage truck must be at the house two doors down. Early-morning dew soaked her shoes as she half ran across the lawn, climbed over the stone wall, skirted the swimming pool and the tennis court, and arrived at the Dilworth garage behind the house just in time. The trash cans were still there—full. The driver of the huge, dirty-gray truck, whom she thought of privately as the garbage man, although he now called himself REFUSE COLLECTOR on his bills, greeted her genially. "Miz Ramsdale, them iris bulbs you give me came up beautiful. I planted 'em like you showed me—reasons on top of the ground."

Lucy translated this correctly as rhizomes. She had reasons of her own for this meeting, and she had no intention of letting them show above ground. "You heard about the awful thing that happened to Miss Dilworth's fiancé two nights ago."

The garbage man exchanged his happy-gardener expression for one more suitable. "Sure sorry about that." He glanced up at a bedroom window, and lowered his voice. "How's she taking it?"

"She's prostrate with shock," Lucy said glibly. "She's staying at my house for a while, and I wondered if you could do us a favor."

The garbage man instantly looked cautious. In his trade, he had learned that doing a favor might entail hauling away anything from a twenty-foot browned-off Christmas tree to a dead skunk. "What did you have in mind?"

"I wondered if you'd just load these trash cans of hers onto your truck and take them over and leave them in my garage?"

Now he looked merely puzzled. "Nobody gonna steal her trash cans while she's gone. Steal almost anything else, these days, but not trash cans."

"The thing is, Miss Dilworth's maid accidentally threw away the only picture of the dead fiancé." Lucy apologized in her head to Zora. "And we're naturally anxious to get it back." At least one of us is. "So I thought if the trash cans were in my garage, I could go through them bit by bit and find the picture."

"Kinda messy job for you."

"I don't mind." Lucy smiled up at him radiantly. She was wearing a delphinium-blue dress that made her eyes even bluer, and she used them full strength. "I knew I could count on you. You're always so thoughtful."

If the garbage man still had doubts, it would have been churlish to express them now. "Hop in and I'll give you a lift back. Grass is still soppy."

163

So Lucy came home in a garbage truck.

Once the cans were safely inside her garage, she put on a long smock and garden gloves and hove to. An empty champagne bottle in the first can she opened nearly broke her resolve. She had a devastatingly clear flash of seeing Grace and Davin, newly engaged, lifting their glasses in a loving toast to the future. But if her hunch was right—and she'd had it with her first cup of coffee, which was the time of some of her best hunches—then the sketch ought to be here. Grace wouldn't have left it in a wastebasket for Zora to find.

She was lucky. The sketch was rammed on top of the trash in the second can she tackled: torn in two—crumpled inside out. Lucy's reaction was a zigzag of indignation and triumph. She had just put the torn pieces into the pocket of her smock when she heard the roar of a car engine outside the garage. She clutched at the pocket and waited trembling, then felt ridiculous as she heard the fat plop of the New York *Times* hitting the front stoop.

With her breakfast, she skim-read the headlines, then froze as she saw on page 5:

DEN MOTHER, DOG FIND BODY
OF MURDERED ARCHITECT

Mrs. Wilbur Trask, den mother of Brownie Scout Troop # 3 of Wingate, Connecticut, took her flock on a cookout and met a new test of the Scout motto BE PREPARED when her dog uncovered the body of a local architect, Fred Thorndike. Mrs. Trask sent her Brownies to alert the police and stood guard with her dog until help arrived. . . .

Lucy's breakfast was ruined. She thought darkly that Janie Trask must have phoned in that story herself to an AP string man. The only comfort was that she herself might soon make headlines, and not relegated to page 5 either.

She had heard McDougal go out very early, soon after she got her hunch, but that had suited her nicely. Now she was ready to track him down. She also wanted to clear out in time to avoid seeing her houseguest.

She managed the latter smoothly by leaving a breakfast tray in the kitchen with a note: "Off to Thrift Shop. See you around noon." It was then eight fifteen, and she wasn't due at the Thrift Shop till nine, so she had plenty of time to find the inspector and stun him with her news.

The only drawback was that McDougal had vanished. He wasn't at headquarters or at Barracks A. He wasn't at Sergeant Terrizi's. "The two of them had breakfast here before seven," Mrs. Terrizi said, "and the inspector ate real good. Three eggs—sausage—he ate like he hadn't had a good meal in weeks."

This impugned Lucy's own cooking to an outrageous degree. She slammed down the receiver in a temper.

She was still in a temper when she got to the Thrift Shop early and stumbled over a large object left in the passageway. The sign on the back door of the shop said: PLEASE LEAVE ALL MERCHANDISE IN HALLWAY *OUTSIDE* THIS DOOR, WITH YOUR NAME AND ADDRESS FIRMLY ATTACHED.

Whoever had left this sizable donation hadn't followed instructions; there was no name or address, firmly attached or otherwise.

The inspector had been at headquarters earlier, and briefly, to talk to Sergeant Bayles. Bayles had listened with a lengthening face and then said, "I'm afraid that's the way it was. Zora must have opened her big mouth. I'll give her hell."

"Don't be too tough on her. She may have been the catalyst."

Sergeant Terrizi made a mental note of one more word he'd have to look up: *catalyst*. (He was spelling it somewhat differently, more like "cat lust.") He was so recharged with ambition that he longed to fill any chinks in his knowledge and go up, up, up. He didn't want to become an inspector, at least not for some years, partly because he didn't believe himself ready, and partly because he wanted to go on working with his reinstated hero. He listened with proprietary pleasure as McDougal went on talking to Bayles: "Let's go over that bicycle timing again from this new angle. If the concert finished at ten, it would take at least fifteen or twenty minutes to clear the building and ensure enough privacy for a meeting in the garden. I think Thorndike may have stayed around longer, inconspicuously, hoping to talk to Foster alone, and then given up after he saw Foster with Lowry. He must have spotted something else as he left, and it bothered him. If Foster and Lowry talked from, say, ten thirty to almost eleven, then X would have needed to get there by ten forty-five at the latest. Would that be possible?"

Bayles said it would. "The road that comes in above Locust Street cuts off almost a mile." He produced a typed list of the times he'd checked on two runs.

"Good. And there wouldn't have been any great need for speed on the return trip." He turned to Sergeant Terrizi, who was already vibrating with eagerness. "Let's test out your first theory right now."

Only a fraction of it had been the sergeant's theory; the inspector had taken that fraction and built it up into an impressive algebraic formula: If X did such and so, then Y would react this way . . . "so what we're looking for ought to be somewhere within that quarter mile."

Once more Terrizi was in the glorious position of unbuckling his lips, like a suggestion box spilling out: "It might be smarter if we parked on the back road and waded across the stream." He grinned. "Not to throw the bloodhounds off our scent, but just so nobody'll spot our car."

"You're right, Sergeant. Lead the way."

They found part of what they were looking for in the woods. Although it was slow, crawling work, the sergeant felt so buoyed up he might have been Mercury kicking up his heels. But he and the inspector, plus two troopers called in as bush beaters, failed, in the end, to turn up the most tangible link in the chain they were forging.

Lucy, from nine to twelve, emptied cartons in the back room of the Thrift Shop, where donations were sorted. She catalogued, among other items, a garnet velvet negligee trimmed with mangy marabou, a forty-year-old set of the *Book of Knowledge*, seventeen pairs of women's chunky-heeled shoes (an infallible sign that chunkies were on the way out), a portable TV with a broken picture tube, and a chamber pot wreathed in forget-me-nots. All of these had the donors' names and addresses attached, and as Thrift Shop volunteers knew from edgy experience, most donors wanted an appraisal for an income-tax deduction: contribution to charity. This had to be handled tactfully, so as to encourage donors to cast more bread upon the waters. Tact, with Lucy, was a sometime thing, but today she refrained from writing on the negligee's appraisal slip, "Junk—50¢." She gave it a generous $5, partly to overcompensate, because she couldn't write out an appraisal slip for the one real bonanza in that day's mixed bag: the donation left anonymously in the hallway, which would fetch anywhere from sixty to a hundred, even secondhand. Odd that the donor wanted to be anonymous. The more Lucy thought about it, the odder it seemed.

One of the fringe benefits of being a Thrift Shop volunteer was that the ladies got first crack at whatever was good, if they wanted to buy it for themselves. Lucy had recently acquired eight crystal wineglasses that way. Now she sat looking thoughtfully at the large, anonymously donated object, then rassled it onto its side and examined it carefully. After she'd found what she'd hoped for, she grabbed a cardboard tag, wrote SOLD! HOLD FOR LUCY RAMSDALE, and tied it firmly in the most conspicuous spot. The three other volunteers noted this act with rolling-eyed interest, and when they went home to lunch they spread the word. By afternoon, tongues were rattling all over town on the subject of Lucy Ramsdale's latest eccentricity.

Zora said to Sergeant Terrizi, "Hi, you caught me just in time. Miss Dilworth told me to go home early again . . . you want to do *what?*"

The ginger pancakes with crab meat filling weren't really left-overs, in Lucy's view, because she had made only a preview sampling from the batter the day before. Today's batch would be even better, and she was exasperated to realize they'd be wasted on Grace, who was wearing a face at half-mast.

"Let's have a drink before lunch."

Grace said she never drank in the middle of the day. "Davin and I always walked five times around the deck before lunch. He said I was the only woman he ever knew who could keep up with him."

Lucy managed to make sympathetic noises before she went back to the kitchen and mixed herself a stiff drink. She then retired to the downstairs bathroom to put on fresh lipstick; she'd bitten off the previous layer in the frustration of having to guard her tongue.

When she rolled the tiered serving cart into the living room, she was startled to see the inspector coming in from the terrace with Grace.

"Have you had lunch? Take this plate and I'll get one for myself. And Mac, get out another snack table."

As McDougal took his first bite of ginger pancake with crab meat, Lucy watched with a creator's tense interest for his reaction. There was none; the inspector might have been swallowing Philadelphia scrapple or soggy blotting paper. Grace wasn't reacting to the food either, but she was certainly reacting—overreacting—to the inspector: "I think it's wonderful of you not to arrest Alec yet, with all that evidence against him. I want to get him a top New York lawyer."

"Most women wouldn't be so fair-minded."

Lucy asked pointedly, "Did you find my note last night?"

"I found it." The inspector smiled at Grace. "And I'm more interested than ever."

Lucy gave him a wait-till-I-get-you-alone look, but he ignored it. Besotted idiot, she thought. She couldn't very well say, "Go out to the garage and reach into the left-hand pocket of my smock. There's a surprise for you," so she tried a more devious approach: "You'll never guess what turned up at the Thrift Shop this morning." The inspector looked bored. "It was left by some anonymous donor—a marvelous English bicycle—a Raleigh—with all kinds of extra gadgets."

"Why, that's the kind Sam and I had. Sam always marked our names on things like that with an engraver's pencil because a thief can't scratch that off, and it gives the police a much better chance of recovering something that's stolen."

"I wish more people would take such intelligent precautions," McDougal said. "Foster's bicycle is missing and he claims it was stolen, but we may never find it."

"Oh, that's the one I gave him after Sam died!"

Lucy had just lifted a bite of pancake to her mouth, and the shock of what Grace was saying made her jab the fork into her cheek. If in trying to help Alec she'd yanked the noose tighter around his neck. . . .

The inspector was saying to Grace, "You've been a great help." He untangled his legs from the snack table that held his almost untouched lunch, and got up. "I'll go right down to the Thrift Shop and check now. If your name's on that bicycle, it may be vital evidence."

You sound like a TV detective who's just learned his lines, Lucy thought sourly.

"You mean evidence to convict Alec?" Grace sounded bewildered. "But why would he want to get rid of a bicycle? I don't understand."

"If he killed Lowry and returned to the Center later to make it look like an accident, Melton or a neighbor would have heard his car going out, but they wouldn't have heard a bicycle. And he could have hidden it easily, right at the Center, whereas a parked car would be noticed."

Grace rubbed her cheek in agitation. "Maybe it was stolen long before this happened. Except that I should think Alec would have told me."

"You've only been home about a week," Lucy said. "And Alec didn't even see you except at the meeting." But he had plenty of chance to tell me, she thought. She had too vivid a picture of Alec two days ago on her terrace, patting his paunch and saying, "I'll have to take up bicycling again." It hadn't been stolen then.

"We'll test the dirt on the wheels. Sergeant Terrizi's found a place in that vacant lot behind the Center where a bicycle may have been stashed while the murderer was busy in the rose garden."

Grace murmured, "It's still too incredible to believe. But if you find my name's on that bicycle, then I'm terribly afraid Alec's involved."

"I'll let you know tonight. And in the meantime, you two look after each other. We're so short of men right now we can't spare any for guard duty—not even a man to watch Foster. I'm hoping he'll decide to talk before he's arrested. He hasn't told all he knows."

Lucy wasn't really listening; she was scratching around in her mind frantically for an excuse to get McDougal alone. "I have an important message for you from Flora Pollit."

The inspector, loping toward the front door, halted beside the phone table and slapped his forehead. He'd forgotten about Flora Pollit. And from what he'd heard of Flora, this had been wishful omission. "What did she say?"

"I can't remember exactly. I wrote it down. It's in the pocket of my—"

The phone rang to cut her off; the inspector reached over and picked up the receiver. Terrizi was supposed to call, and he hoped this was the sergeant.

It was. "Yes, fine, I'm glad you got that taken care of. And I think we've located the bicycle. Meet me at the Thrift Shop. . . . I'm leaving right now."

As he hung up, Grace came from the other end of the room. "I thought it might be my maid calling."

"No, it was for me." He remembered one other stop he had to make on the way into Wingate, and he said to Lucy impatiently, "Where's the message?"

"I'll get it." But how could she produce the smock with Grace standing right there? Ask Mac to go out to the garage with her? But who left messages in a garage? And if Grace tagged along to goo at the inspector. . . .

McDougal thought, She can't even remember which memo pad she wrote it on. "Never mind. I'll get it later."

He strode out the door and was already in his car when Lucy

came running after him, waving and making wild motions, practically throwing herself in his path as he drove off.

"Can't stop now," he yelled. Seen in his rearview mirror, Lucy abandoned in the driveway, looked so small and so open-mouthed incredulous that he felt rather mean. To appease his conscience, at his next stop he called Flora Pollit.

After her torrential introductory trivia on why she had had to leave town early Thursday morning "to attend an important conference on the polluting of the Connecticut River," he was ready to dry up the source when she finally came to the point, or at least pattered around it. "A friend insisted on driving me home after the concert, but I still hadn't done my three-mile stint —I do believe walking is the greatest exercise of all—so I just put my Ralphie on a leash—I named him after Ralph Nader—and Ralphie and I went walking."

"Where did you go, Miss Pollit?"

"That's what I wanted to tell you. I was still very upset by Mr. Lowry's proposals for the rose garden. The pieces of sculpture he showed us slides of were totally alien to the tradition of Wingate, and I do feel that to accept the sewage of art is as evil as pouring industrial waste into rivers. . . ."

"So you went back to look at the pieces of sculpture that had already been uncrated?" the inspector asked prayerfully.

"I wish I had." Her listener swallowed a groan. "But as Ralphie and I were coming down Locust—that's the street behind the Center and not well lit at all—I saw this sinister figure get off a bicycle—very tall and dark and furtive with his cap pulled way down. He stuck his bicycle into some bushes and slunk through the vacant lot toward the rose garden. So naturally I didn't want to encounter so unpleasant a character—he was definitely a criminal type—and I thought of calling the police when I got home, but they have been shockingly neglectful in following up other leads I've given them, on dumpers of empty beer cans—so I refused to give such vital information to anyone but you. There is no doubt in my mind I saw the degenerate who killed Davin Lowry."

The inspector said she'd done exactly the right thing in calling him. "And I'll tell you something in darkest confidence"—he rather fancied that "in darkest confidence"—"because I know I can rely on your discretion." (Or lack of it.) "Alec Foster has admitted he met Lowry in the garden late that night, and he also admits hiding Fred Thorndike's body. The evidence against him is so overwhelming we'll have to arrest him tonight."

"But—but it couldn't have been Alec I saw. He's inches shorter, and—"

"I realize that. Obviously there must have been a conspiracy. For 'conspiracy' read 'frame-up.' My lips are sealed for the nonce, even with you." He was afraid *nonce* was going too far, but Flora Pollit didn't seem to think so. She breathed heavily and said of course she understood.

The inspector was twenty minutes late getting to the Thrift Shop. When he drove into the parking lot in the rear, a beaming Terrizi came to meet him. "It's the bicycle, all right. Her name's under the handlebar." The sergeant didn't mention the tag attached to the handlebar—HOLD FOR LUCY RAMSDALE—because there had been no tag when he saw it. A volunteer on the afternoon shift had removed it gladly when Lucy called and said she'd changed her mind about taking up bicycling. A pair of imported hickory skis had come in that very hour, and the volunteer said to her coworkers, "Girls, let's try to sell these before Lucy Ramsdale lays eyes on them."

The inspector finished telling Terrizi about Flora Pollit's "degenerate." "So that helps, but as a witness she'd turn off any jury. We need more evidence, and this is the way we'll set the trap. . . ."

16

The portrait of Sam in the lobby seemed even more pervasive today. Not just the jawbone jutting at her, but now the eyes seemed to shine from their sockets like distress signals.

Sam, I can't help it, Lucy said silently. If Grace is guilty, I can't let her get away with it. I have to tell Alec about the sketch and try to find out if he's protecting Grace or somebody else. If Grace is innocent, I'll try to like her again. She turned her back on Sam and marched resolutely toward the closed door of Alec's office, then halted to add a defiant P.S.: But no matter how many mobile lab units she buys the police with your damn money, I won't let her marry the inspector.

At the moment, Lucy thought McDougal almost deserved that fate. She was still indignant over the way he'd behaved, practically running her down in her own driveway. And that patronizing speech he'd made about "You two women stay together and look after each other." Not that Grace had paid any attention to it either; she had said she was going back to her house to pick up more clothes. Lucy said she wanted to do some marketing. As soon as Grace had gone, she'd checked on the smock in the garage to make sure the sketch was still there. Then she got out her shopping bag, went back upstairs, and collected one accessory for her errand.

She had to shift the shopping bag to the other arm to turn the doorknob of Alec's office, and the empty desk with the poster for macramé classes, ALL KNOTTED UP? seemed, in her present mood, entirely too pertinent. She made a mean face at it, sat down in the only spare chair, and debated whether to go to the Thrift Shop to find Mac. After the inspector's cavalier treatment, she felt he really didn't deserve her help for a while. Eventually, perhaps this evening, she'd show him the sketch that had been so savagely crumpled and torn.

The thought of a chastened, embarrassed McDougal was delicious, until a new doubt assailed her like indigestion. She remembered she'd known several widows and widowers who couldn't bear any photograph of the dead loved one around; they found it too harrowing. If Grace had suddenly felt that way about the sketch of Davin and crumpled it in a hysterical moment but hadn't wanted to hurt Lucy's feelings by telling her, then the evidence culled from the trash can was exactly nil. After all, it was Alec who'd made the sneak date with Davin in the rose garden, and Alec who now owned the bicycle, and Alec who'd dumped Fred Thorndike's body. . . .

As Lucy ticked off these worrying points, she heard the door behind her open slowly and felt as if an ice cube had been slid down her back.

"Oh, Mrs. Ramsdale! I didn't know anybody was here."

Martha Teague came trotting in, her thonged sandals making a *slappeta* sound on the hardwood floor.

Lucy was so relieved she was almost effusive in her greeting. Martha's round-and-round braids were a tilting bird's nest, and her face was blotchy, as if she'd been crying. "I'm so glad to see you because I know you're a real friend of Alec's. You *don't* think he's guilty, do you?"

Lucy said she hoped he wasn't. Once again her confidence surged up so strongly she added, "And I may have a lead to the real murderer."

Martha Teague didn't seem to hear. "Did you know they're going to arrest Alec later today? Flora Pollit told me in strictest confidence. I've been so upset I've been doing macramé—you know, knotting—because when I do things with my hands it helps calm me." She pulled a long woven strip out of her handbag.

"It's the lutestring choker. Isn't it pretty? I've been trying to fasten it on myself to see where the ties should start. But it's for my oldest grandchild, and her neck's so dainty, like yours. Would you mind if I just tried it on you for size?"

Lucy raised her head, humoring this pitiful woman. Martha Teague stood behind her and slipped the choker around. As Lucy felt it tighten she had the flashing recall of a drowning man: *Grandchild—Martha's grandchild blinded—Martha objecting so emotionally to the sharp prongs of "Moon God"—a child might get hurt. . . .* The choker tightened even more; Lucy thrashed her legs wildly and tried to scream.

"Mrs. Ramsdale, are you having a seizure or something? Oh, where, oh, where are those smelling salts?"

The pressure on Lucy's Adam's apple blessedly eased as the choker slid onto her shoulder. Martha was scrabbling through her handbag. "I used them on Mrs. Voorhies after she sniffed the gold leaf, but I thought I put them back into—oh, here. This will fix you."

An uncorked phial was rammed under Lucy's nose; the reek of ammonia assaulted her nostrils and stung her eyes till tears streamed.

"There, isn't that better? I couldn't imagine what had come over you."

"Much better," Lucy gasped. "You pulled the lutestrings a little too tight."

"Oh, how clumsy of me. But I've been in such a state of nerves. Alec told me if he was taken to jail I should weave him a rope so he could dangle it out of his cell window and shinny down like Rapunzel backward. He was trying to make me laugh." Martha Teague made a hiccupy sobbing sound. "But I don't feel like laughing, do you?"

Lucy massaged her throat and said truthfully, no, she didn't. "Where's Alec now?"

"He said he was going to stay home this afternoon. I told Miss Dilworth a little while ago she could find him there."

Lucy felt ice cold again. Grace wouldn't go to see Alec unless she knew he wasn't the murderer. And the only way Grace could know for sure. . . . "Martha, get the Thrift Shop and ask for Inspector McDougal." While Martha dialed, Lucy reached across the desk for a memo pad.

"It's busy. I'll try again in a minute."

Lucy was already scribbling frantically. "Tell him I'm going to Alec's right now. And if anything happens to me, give him this note." She scrawled a last sentence: *Look in left-hand pocket of smock in garage—I got it out of Grace's garbage can.*

"The line's still busy."

"Can't wait." Lucy swung up her shopping bag. In the doorway, she paused. "Call and warn Alec."

Martha said nervously, "Warn him about what?"

Well, what? Better not mention Grace. Lucy said, "The murderer," which seemed ambiguous enough. She took off like a small tornado.

As she backed out the Saab, she felt an ominous jolt and settling; damn fireplug, rear fender stuck on it. She shifted gears, stepped down hard on the gas, and heard the grinding wrench as the little car pulled free and leaped ahead like a rabbit sprung from a trap.

She made the three miles from Wingate to the house next to Alec's in just over three minutes, and she made the turn into her neighbors' driveway at roughly the same speed, but overshot the driveway and plowed across the lawn. As she jumped out with her shopping bag, she had one rueful glimpse of the track her tires had dug across the exquisitely tended lawn. Her neighbors, a New York couple named Vosburgh, only came up on Friday evenings for weekends; with luck, she'd get her car out before they arrived and make her peace with them later. If I'm alive to apologize, she thought.

With belated caution, she ducked down so that her head wouldn't show above the hedge between the two houses while she crept around to the back, still lugging her shopping bag, and went through the opening to Alec's.

His little Japanese car was parked in the rear driveway beside the small, closed garage, looking so trim and untouched, especially compared to Lucy's battered Saab, that she felt suddenly idiotic, skulking around like the last of the Mohicans. She straightened up, groaned as her back muscles creaked, and stood in the tranquil shade of a giant ash tree for a moment to cool off. Then she walked around to the front door and knocked. The silence made her uneasy all over again. She tried the door, found it was unlocked, and went in, calling "Alec." Each room she went through had the flat emptiness of a stage set. She ended up in the kitchen and went out the back door, thinking, Have to go back and collect my car and go over to Grace's to see if Alec's there. Even the thought of walking the few hundred feet again made her feel so shaky she leaned against the side of the garage—and heard a woman's voice, harsh as a blow: "Don't try to reach that rake with your foot. I'm a crack shot."

"This rope around my hands is too tight. It's stopped the circulation."

"Good. I'll stop it dead. Then nobody will know about Davin. I knew he was lying about the slides. I saw him put them in his pocket after the meeting. He was going in to meet someone, and I had to find out who. So I borrowed your bicycle."

A mumble Lucy couldn't make out, then Grace again: "No, but I heard enough. You wanted him to tell me before we were married. And he said he'd leave me a note saying he wasn't the marrying kind and go off. He couldn't be honest with me even then."

This time, Alec's voice came out more clearly: ". . . blame myself for interfering . . . obsessed because of my sister."

Harsh laugh from Grace. "As if I'd ever be like your sister. Nobody puts one over on Sam Dilworth's daughter. Davin found that out soon enough."

"He really loved you." Alec again. "He must have thought he could change."

"But *you* didn't think he could change. You thought he'd have to sneak off and have boys on the side. And then I'd come home some day and find him in bed with—"

"No!" It was a sharp cry. "He might never have slipped. A lot of men don't, once they're married."

"Men! He was a scheming pansy. And you're another."

"I didn't turn you in to the police. Even after I realized you must have killed him, I felt so responsible."

"But you'd turn me in to save your own neck. I had to get to you before they arrested you. And now you'll drive your car into the garage and you'll be found here dead, with the motor running. Suicide. Everybody will think you were the killer. They already found out you dumped Fred's body. Served you right for being so clever."

"Why did you have to kill Fred too?"

"He was here on the terrace when I brought the bicycle back. He'd come to see me that night after he saw you and Davin together, and I wasn't at home, but later I told the police I was. And then when Fred saw me arrive with the bicycle, he—" Her voice sharpened. "You're stalling for time. I have to kill you before anybody comes. Then I'll be in the clear. The inspector's crazy about me, and Lucy's an addled old fool."

Lucy had been frozen in position with her ear to the garage wall, and her discomfort seemed to blend with her terror for Alec into one numbing physical pain that drained all her strength. Now the shock of hearing herself described as an addled old fool pumped her adrenalin fast. Damn Mac—he wasn't going to get here in time. She reached into her shopping bag, got out her new flashlight, and pressed the siren button hard.

As it wailed deafeningly, she ran to the front of the garage, yelling, "Police!"

The garage door slid up before she could get the flashlight back into her bag, so she held it behind her.

Alec stood in the opening, his hands tied together with clothesline, and a dumfounded look on his face. "Lucy! You shouldn't have come."

Under the circumstances, it seemed an inadequate statement. Grace appeared from the dim interior holding a gun.

"I told you she was a fool. Now I'll have to kill her too."

"You haven't time," Lucy said. "The police are on their way in. Grace, you'd better run for the woods." She tried to press the siren button again, behind her back, but hit the flashlight button instead and a long, pale beam of light streaked across the drive-way.

Grace burst out laughing. "Remember the first night you used it when I came for your car? I was terrified—I thought the police must have trailed me from the Center. How sweet of you to explain your gadget to me then. I'll get Alec's prints on it and then I'll use it to bash your head in." She strode out and rammed the gun into Lucy's side. "Get in there with Alec."

"She's not going." The inspector had appeared suddenly from the far side of the garage, and he was aiming a gun straight at Grace.

"Come one step closer and I'll kill Lucy."

"I'm happy to tell you that's impossible. Sergeant Terrizi took the bullets out of your gun early this afternoon."

Grace said in almost a croon, "So I discovered. Sam always made me check on my ammunition."

The inspector strolled toward her. "Luckily, the sergeant took away all your extra bullets."

"That's what *he* thought. I hid some after the police began to get so nosy. This gun is loaded. If you come any closer, I'll demonstrate."

Lucy felt Grace's gun prod her and cried, "Mac, I don't think she's bluffing."

"If you kill Lucy Ramsdale and Alec," the inspector said, "then you'll have to kill me too. How will you explain that away?"

"I'll make it look as if Alec killed all of you."

"The police won't buy that. Terrizi knows all about you."

"I'll get the best lawyers in the country. Temporary insanity."

"You just might get away with it. But more probably you'd be locked up in a mental institution. I think you'd find it confining."

His tone was so conversational Lucy felt like screaming, This is no time for a chat.

The leaves of the big ash tree seemed to be trembling, and she thought, I'm dizzy—I mustn't faint. She closed her eyes, opened them, and saw the leaves over Grace's head trembling even more, but now she saw why.

"Oh, Grace, you'd hate being locked up," she babbled. "You couldn't ride or swim—"

"Or shoot," Alec said *sotto voce*.

"But if you'd bribe the inspector," Lucy said wildly. "Those mobile lab units you were talking about—you might easily buy your way out if—"

Terrizi hurtled out of the tree just as McDougal flung himself forward and pushed Lucy away. A gun cracked, and the inspector fell like a log.

Grace hadn't been bluffing.

17

The inspector's hospital bed was cranked up just enough to make it impossible for him to lie down or sit up decently straight.

Lucy, pushing the door open a few inches with her foot, saw that the dinner tray on the trolley table across the bed seemed to be almost under his chin.

She marched in, carrying a large covered basket á la Little Red Riding Hood. "Would it hurt your side if I cranked you up?"

"It only hurts when I curse," the inspector said. "I've been cursing most of the day." An invalid pallor had muted his tan, and his long, bony face wore the Rouault suffering-eye-socket look: this brightened considerably as he took in the covered basket.

"I meant to get here by five thirty, but Nicky Terrizi caught me again just as I was leaving. Have you already eaten?"

"I took one bite. The chicken tastes like watered-down rooster."

Lucy put down her basket, lifted the hospital tray, and put it on a side table as if she were disposing of a dead rat. She cranked up the bed, whisked the napkin off her basket, took out a small thermos jug, a plate, and various plastic containers. "Veal birds, romaine with sour-cream-and-caviar dressing. . . ." She went on doling out a feast.

The inspector knew what he ought to say but couldn't think how to say it, so instead, he ate. And ate.

With dessert, which was strawberry tart, he had recovered enough to mutter, "I should really be eating crow."

"I looked up my recipe for crow, but it takes too damn long to cook. And after all, you did save my life, more or less."

McDougal shifted position, put his hand to his bandaged side, and groaned.

"Psychosomatic pain," Lucy said. "After all, Grace's gun wasn't loaded." She gave a not-very-ladylike snort. "The next time you choose partners for Russian roulette, count Alec and me out."

"Alec showed a lot of guts," the patient said humbly. "I'd asked him to keep her talking till we learned exactly why she killed Thorndike. And she did. A good thing, too, because now she refuses to talk to anybody but her high-priced New York lawyer. We already know why she pushed Lowry downstairs."

"I thought she soaped the steps so he'd slip."

"She did that afterward. I think she pushed Lowry in a rage and then tried to make it look as if he'd slipped and fallen. The pathologist who did the autopsy discovered—" He stopped abruptly. "It's not pretty."

"You'd better tell me. Look what happened before when you tried to fool me. I told you Grace wasn't the girl for you, and you said 'I'm more interested than ever.'"

"Well, I was, once I realized she might be the killer."

"It took you long enough."

"You'd confused the issue—you and your matchmaking. I made the mistake of trusting your judgment. 'Nice wholesome million-airess next door, just wants to use her money to make a husband happy.' Ha."

"We all make mistakes," Lucy said, in her most gracious tone. "What made you finally catch on?"

"I remembered what she'd said about your having ears like a fox. She *wanted* you to hear her take out your car, because she knew then you'd get me involved and I'd be with her when we found Lowry's body. I'd see the heartbroken fiancée, bravely accepting tragedy. I was a sucker to fall for that one." He lit a cigarette, but it tasted so awful he put it out.

"No, because she wasn't just acting. I think she really was in agony. If she'd pushed Davin in a sudden rage, she couldn't have meant to kill him."

"Well, she did afterward. Lowry wasn't killed outright by the fall. That's what I started to tell you. When Grace found he was unconscious but still breathing, she must have rammed his head harder onto the prongs and—"

Lucy shut her eyes and looked sick. "Don't tell me."

The inspector started to say, You asked for it, but when he saw how pale she was, he said quickly, "She *was* lying about your having a bad heart, wasn't she?" He repeated the excuse Grace had given him for not phoning to ask if she might borrow Lucy's car.

Lucy was healthily indignant. "Trying to make me into an old crock. That is really too much."

"There's another thing I've been wanting to check with you. The day after Lowry's murder, did Grace talk to her maid on the phone and then make some excuse to go right back to her house?"

Lucy nodded.

"Zora let slip that I'd given Sergeant Bayles a funny assignment—to go bicycling. So that's when Grace knew I wasn't taken in by Davin's 'accidental fall' and she had to get home in a hurry and take the bicycle away. She'd borrowed it that night while Alec and Bert were still at the Center, and she'd hidden it in her basement afterward because she couldn't take a chance on returning it just then. But as soon as she knew we suspected murder, she had to return the bicycle and start building up evidence against Alec. Alec found it on the terrace near Fred's body, but he didn't realize till later the bicycle would incriminate him. That's when he took it around to the Thrift Shop. So Zora started quite a chain reaction with her slip."

"Grace told me she had to get home right away to see if the sketch of Davin would fit a silver frame." Lucy looked slightly flustered. "I should have showed you the sketch first, but it wouldn't have meant anything then. He looked pettish, but you often look pettish yourself."

The inspector swallowed hard. If he was getting a dose of his own medicine, he was inclined to think he should take it like a man and even lick the spoon. "Bert Melton certainly isn't pettish. He came to see me this noon to thank me. And he brought me that plant." He tried to keep out of his voice any hint of his private conviction that men didn't bring flowers to another man, not under any circumstances.

Lucy said demurely, "He knows how much you like flowers."

The patient's Adam's apple bobbled again. "It was very decent of him. You know, he'd suspected Grace before any of us did— even before Alec—and he wanted to go and have it out with her. I put an extra guard on their house late the night Thorndike was killed and I had Bert tailed all yesterday to make sure he wouldn't get in Grace's way and she couldn't get at him."

"You didn't hesitate to leave *me* alone with her."

"Because I knew as long as you didn't suspect anything, you were safe."

"That's like saying, 'You may keep a rattlesnake as a house pet as long as you don't poke it in the mouth and say "Open wide."'"

"Thank God you didn't tackle her right after you found that sketch. Terrizi told me how you dug it out of the garbage can. That was—er—brilliant detective work."

"A lot more brilliant than Janie Trask letting her dog stumble over a body."

"Yes, I saw that story about Mrs. Trask in the *Times*." McDougal's mouth quirked slightly at the corners. "But I think you'll find tomorrow's *Times* much more interesting. You and Terrizi both. You were the ones who really solved the case. I would have told the TV men that too, but I was damned if I'd let them bring in their cameras and shoot me in a hospital bed."

"You could give them a statement," Lucy said. Her dark blue eyes glinted greedily. "I usually listen to Walter Cronkite."

"Listen tomorrow night," the inspector said recklessly. Then he frowned. "But if you wanted to bring in my dinner again, you could listen to the news right here in my room." He indicated the television set suspended from the wall at a cosy tilt designed to keep patients from craning and to drive visiting viewers cross-eyed.

184

"All right. Which would you rather have—fish stew or more of the beef bourguignon?"

The inspector had sudden total recall: Lucy making the hideous face as she stirred the beef dish. "Why were you standing at the stove making a face?"

"Oh, you mean like this?" Lucy stuck out her tongue—*yanh, yanh, yanh.*

The nurse who had come in to pick up the dinner tray was shocked.